MOHAMMED
a mechanic
& MARY
a maid

MOHAMMED
a mechanic
& MARY
a maid

And other stories of *Dusky India*

B L GAUTAM

PARTRIDGE
A Penguin Random House Company

To order additional copies of this book, contact
Partridge India
000 800 10062 62
www.partridgepublishing.com/india
orders.india@partridgepublishing.com

CONTENTS

MOHAMMED A MECHANIC
AND MARY A MAID

Pet hate is a sign of affection. It's like a baby cry—'don't leave me alone; take me in your arms'. And it may take a life time, perhaps more, for the hug to happen.

Mohan Batteries is not a place it was to be. Once a favourite spot for taxi-drivers to recharge their car batteries, now gives a desolate look. It's no more a destination to fix the recurring faults of over-used cars. The Premier car—everyone calls it Fiat still—was at one time an everywhere vehicle of Bombay. The wrecked 4-wheeler is stubbornly around; not willing to call it a day. It's an embarrassment first, then a car, but as yellow-and-black taxi it still dominates the scene. Premier Auto shut shop long back. New age batteries don't ask maintenance. A car defines the owner's status today.

Owner of Mohan Batteries, Rajesh Bajaj was first a fixer, and then anything else. He was. Now he's one irritated old ass. He visits his shop, off and on. There's hardly a work. He hasn't yet stopped nursing the dream of turning his twenty-by-ten shop into a lottery outlet or something that needs no watch. Mohan Batteries with its weathered signboard sits an unhappy structure in this bustling area.

Bajaj believes no work is worth him. His cronies of teeming times have deserted him for greener pastures. Once in a while, you see a familiar face hesitantly releasing a smile of acquaintance.

Everything's changed, except Mohammed. Mohammed is what he was. Gone grey but his agility is the same. Footprints of the bygone are untraceable on his stoical face. Work or no work, you will find him around. Although the name Mohammed doesn't float in the air like it once did.

Neither considered a good mechanic nor a safe driver still that's what he is—a mechanic plus driver. You can't simply dismiss a person who's always pleased to tend the apology you own as a car. And in today's world where do you get a driver anytime ready to take charge of your wheel.

A time was, customer or idler, everyone looked for Mohammed. Mohammed was perpetually busy. Either half shoved into the bonnet of a car or lying underneath as if struggling to come out of its womb. His greasy garb made him look like a newly born, un-bathed child of an automobile. He really has no idea of his parents.

If not charging a battery or checking a car, he would be gone out to get something for someone from somewhere. Mohammed never grumbled even when he should have. There was a reason to it. His job was to do what he was asked to. It made his livelihood. He realized this soon after he learned to walk. He was not paid for everything he did. But he would be, he believed.

Light, agile and restless—comes at his first look. Never happy, and never sad; he always had, and still has that lost look on his face. Nothing excites and nothing troubles him much. It appears.

How could one be so hopelessly occupied? It's amazing. Completely unaware of what is going around him. He could easily be taken a dope. But no, Mohammed has been a teetotaller all through his life. He also eats very less. Necessity quietly becomes habit. He is fond of nothing. Fondness comes with choice. He never had. Not choice, give him a piece of work if you have. That's what he needs. Of course for money. But money will follow when there is work. He believes.

Officers of Customs and their wives in the nearby colony had always something that Mohammed should do, could do, and would do. They had helluva money. So much that some of it was always spilling around. In those days of no plastic money, no credit cards, no expensive cars and gadgets—a bundle of few thousands always in the side pocket was what people called big money. A Customs officer would always have it— stop and check. It was a common knowledge of every shop-keeper and vendor on Wadala Station Road. These rapid rich were far more benevolent than those traditional squirrels. Money that comes from hidden sources gets spent through open channels mostly. Funny! And curiously, it's not the user's decision. It is perhaps the hidden momentum in such currency that makes it pass through so many hands so fast.

Those who didn't have it called it black money. For Mohammed, it came in such small quantities in return of so long hours of toiling that in the journey it would regain the original colour. Less or more than he expected, sooner or later than he thought, every one paid him for the work he did.

Harish Chandra Negi would never step out of his house with less than five thousand bucks in his pocket; a little more was more elevating. Whenever he told Mohammed to do anything—wash the car, check oil, get a *tandoori* chicken from Koliwada or salad and soda from Wadala market—a note of hundred was coming, Mohammed knew. Hundred rupees were like a week's earnings for Mohammed. He found it really disproportionate and always looked for to do something, before Mr Negi asks for. Wiping his car or tuning up the engine or anything in order to even out. At least in his mind.

Negi was an Assistant Commissioner of Customs and in those days of pre-liberalisation the post was bigger than what's generally considered big in government service. Power, money, and some share of glamour came as assured benefits if one was posted at international airport. Negi was.

Mrs Negi, popularly Tara madam, was a senior officer of Sales Tax. As in-charge of Nasik division she kept at the divisional circuit house through the weekdays. On weekends she was always in Mumbai to spend time with her husband. Position and money, no doubt, bring a stress at the domestic front. But it's worth till the perks are on. Their only son, Rohit, was in Solan Public School, close to Negi's native place. This weekly union of Mr and Mrs Negi reassured the durability of their marital bond. Sex was a stamp.

Mohammed was at times so taken over by Harish Negi that he had no time for others. Rajesh Bajaj would intently listen and then sweetly ignore the whines of his other benefactors for Mohammed's unavailability. The lure of chicken and Black Label, and if the kick was great, a visit to some infamous dance bar was enough to silence his inner conflict. Black Label was big bait. It could easily earn you a decent half an hour with a minister or the police commissioner to narrate your woes in detail. It was good enough to pocket a well-known reporter for a day, if one had a dream to see his face on a tabloid. Cognoscenti often said, 'What money can't BL can'. Why to blame Bajaj then. The poor guy was no more than a parasitic louse lost in Johnny Walker's pubic region.

Mohammed was happy to be a help to Tara madam no matter she was not benevolent like her husband. For anything he did, she would never give him more than ten bucks, irrespective of his time and toil. At times, he would wait while she searched for the change. He always needed money but wouldn't mind if carried forward. In such dealings, accumulated obligation is more than the sum of its parts. She hardly kept it pending, anyway. Mohammed respected her to-the-point interaction. Actually that is a more decent way to deal with a servant than always taking a dig to create a sense of warmth. Pay him his dues, keep the sympathy aside. For special occasions.

It was Mary, their maid, Mohammed loathed most. Mary and Mohammed could never get along. To Mohammed's aversion, she never treated him equal, and that she ought to have if nothing more. If he did odd jobs for Negis, so what, she too was a maid to them. The difference was she got wages and he received what's snobbishly called a 'tip'. But had you asked Mary, this tip thing was a defining difference.

When Mary needed something urgently, she would pick up the phone and ask Mohammed in a tone that was distinctly belittling. She was using that command on behalf of Harish Negi, Mohammed knew. He always argued for a while. Not on a point but in defence of his self respect. He had to do what Mary asked for, the bugger knew jolly well. He would never miss a chance to give it partly back by snubbing her. He had nothing to do with her pretty face or her curvaceous body; an object of desire for every idler at Mohan Batteries.

Mary was a widow. Her husband, a Municipality worker, a drunkard, a Marathi-speaking protestant like herself, passed away quietly in his alcohol-induced sleep on an otherwise fine day. She mourned for few days, and everything was normal, faster than normally it is. The credit goes to penury that wouldn't allow the luxury of lazing around in the pall of grief.

That was three years back. Mary worked as a maid before she got married, continued to be one during the short spell of marital bliss, and was a maid still. She changed a few employers on the way. Housemaid is one of those unique professions where more often a servant chooses the employer. Soon after attaining the widowhood she came to Negis, and sooner she was a part of the household. She was pleasant, smart, and pretty good at her work.

If Rajesh Bajaj was sure that you were not in direct touch with Negi, he had no qualms speaking out his mind—'What a sexy doll boss! Have you properly seen her butt?'

He would look into your eyes to scan your imagination. Not convinced, he would stand up and describe animatedly, 'Look at the breasts, tight and shapely. Think of her hips and I bet you will have an instant erection. When she walks up to the colony, many pair of eyes escort her until she enters the gate and disappears. This limping bastard—he would point to the locksmith slotted in a corner—keeps gazing at her, vigorously rotating the key in the hole.'

'Negi must be visiting heaven at least once a day. No?' One of his cronies would hungrily dig.

'You are an idiot', before releasing his punch, Bajaj would give a look that could easily be mistaken as angst by a novice, 'you can't visit the place you live in, you mother-fucker.' That was a moment for a burst of laughter Bajaj would nonchalantly accept as ovation.

Rajesh Bajaj had seen the duet of adulterous looks between Harish Negi and Mary during those long binge sessions at Negi's house. In side-glances, she would often show that wife-type annoyance if Negi crossed the limit of three drinks or if he failed to instantly turn down his friends' proposal for a dinner at some oft-mentioned restaurant, or sometimes for his over-indulgence into those man jokes. A man of Bajaj's experience would rarely miss those signs. To his eye of a rascal, it was a lingering flair; the subtext of the latest 'bedtime' story. To his seasoned fixer, it was cool, 'only a fool will pay for the milk and feed a cow.'

Mohammed often overheard the juicy comments about this scandalous relationship, but never thought much. Life's wicked games were not for his indulgence. To him life existed between problems and solutions, faults and repairs. Beyond that everything was a luxury, unaffordable to him. Who fucks who was none of his business? He never carried that unnecessary baggage; the reason behind his agile and detached demeanour, perhaps.

To Rajesh Bajaj, Mohammed was a bastard of another degree. That was evident from his remarks whenever Mohammed would leave a job half way for his Friday prayers.

'This fucker also goes for *namaz*; look at him. Who is he making a fool of? I knew him when he worked at Moosa's garage at Antop Hill. He was some fucking D' Souza. Moosa called him Gabby. Only to marry, he changed his religion. He doesn't know a word of Quran.'

To Mohammed, it didn't matter. He really didn't know a word of Quran and that too didn't matter much to him.

Mohammed had a mechanical mind; serviceable. He would never carry along a problem. 'Fix it and restart' was his way of life. Only one occurrence has lingered on his memory for years. It is like a slight yet visible dent that never gets repaired.

It has been twenty years since then. His wife is still his wife but only on the ration card. The wife, to get possession of her, he changed his religion. He became Mohammed from Gabriel De Souza. His only daughter got married when they were together. She is happy with her husband. Mohammed has three sons, one from him and two he got with the woman. All three are working now. None of them comes to meet him. No regrets. He never expected so much from life. He is still not sad. Neither happy.

He has in fact no fascination for the flashbacks of his life. He keeps himself busy. He is now more into fixing metallic logos, and fancy accessories, on variety of new age cars. Not an exciting job for him but a recent addition to his skill-set. He gets them from *chor bazaar*. He knows these fixtures are flicked from other cars. Theft, it's.

Mary encourages him to do this, for quicker and better returns. To see Mohammed sulking, she has only one thing to say, 'Let the thieves do their job, and you do yours. Those whose sell these to you know what they are doing and those who buy these from you know it still better. You don't make these items at home. And you are also not one who steals them. You pay for them. Be good but change yourself for the better.'

Mary's short sermon was enough to make Mohammed cautious of not making his dislike for the job ever visible.

She is now his woman, completely in charge of his life. Mohammed now lives with Mary; visits his wife only when he has some money or clothes to give. Sometimes Mary sends with him a pail of chicken curry. Mohammed takes it as her good-heartedness. She does it for her love for Mohammed.

It all began with the day Negi and his wife went to their native place on vacation. For upkeep of the house, they left the key with their trusted maid.

Before leaving, Harish Negi called up Mohammed and briefed him right in front of Mary, 'Fetch her whatsoever she needs in our absence.' His tone was admonishing. Negi took out three notes of hundred rupees, handed it out to Mohammed with a rebuke, 'Keep it. She is like your sister. You should take care of her.'

While shoving the notes into his pocket Mohammed was figuring out whether it was the biggest 'tip' of his life or it was to get something for Mary if she asked for or a bribe to accept her as his sister. His mechanic's mind couldn't deal with the thought for long. But he was convinced that whatever he had heard about Negi's relationship with Mary was all true. He didn't know how he was convinced so much, so suddenly. But he was.

He dropped Negi and his wife to the airport, brought their Fiat back, parked it and went to their house to hand over the car key to Mary. He anticipated trouble, some altercation, but gathered his nerve to face it. He could see the door was ajar. He peeped in. An open bottle of Coke sat on the table.

He spoke loudly, 'The key is on the table.'

'Wait! coming!' Mary was louder, stern too.

She came out in a gown that was Tara madam's. She had just taken her bath. She had a soft pink towel tied around her head. It was certainly Tara madam's. An overwhelming fragrance enveloped them together. The fragrance was also Tara madam's, Mohammed could make out.

To take her seat, she walked around the sofa-set, like she owned it. Cosiness was hers as she sat. While making her claim, she made her un-caged breasts wallop and hips swing uninhibitedly. The strutting was not to entice him; Mohammed had a brainwave. It was to clear the doubt he had in his mind. It was to make an emphatic statement, *Yes Mohammed, I sleep with Negi.*

The command I exercise upon you is not a whim of my mind. I have a licence to it.'

He hardly looked at her.

'Take this coke. This is for you only.' Mohammed's discomfiture was her fun.

'Wait, I will get something to eat for you.' She got up and went into the kitchen. Now came the turn of her pretty butt to make a statement as she flailed it for him—*'I am too sexy for you. But let me have you an eyeful of my treasure, you dumb'.*

'Have a good look, idiot. I have heard the gushes of many bastards. You know this fortune is not yours. But have some courage to make a remark.'

It was enough to unsettle Mohammed. He guzzled down the full bottle in two attempts and went out of the house before she was back from the kitchen.

Mary would think twice before calling him on his shop's number that was answered by a different voice every time. A woman asking for Mohammed, every now and then, could be a free fun for the bunch of scoundrels warming their ass.

During this interlude, Mohammed kept himself away from her sight to keep the trouble away. He did his best and succeeded, till he got a message from another maid from the colony that Mary was sick and needed some pills from the chemist.

This is a fucking trap, Mohammed fretted. He was losing his cool mechanical approach to things happening around him. A troubled mind was a problem Mohammed had no clue how to handle. He would opt to ignore it like a yelping puppy that calms down when no reaction comes from the passer-by. This illness was an excuse, he suspected. Yet the worry kept popping up—*'what if she is really unwell'*. And if she tells of his callous response to Negi; a hassle was wrapped up to be delivered. The picture of 'Gandhi' on the notes, with his half mouth open and a genuine smile crossed his mind. Money was no issue; it comes somehow, if you stick on. This 'sister thing' was not done, uncalled for, Mohammed resented. *'You sleep with her; what I have to do. Why have you to fuck 'my sister', Bastard!'*

He was yielding slowly. Before catching up with it, he juggled with the thought of visiting her in the afternoon, once free from work.

A sense of guilt suddenly swept him as he saw Mary. She looked really tormented. She was in bed it seemed for a few days. A faint but un-injured smile emerged on her face like a safe survivor of a mishap.

Etiquette was unknown to Mohammed. Without enquiring about her health, he asked, 'Give me the slip for your medicine.'

Mary gave a long stare to skim the simple and unreadable person she was trying to read for quite some time. Focussed on his face she spoke, 'No, I have got the pills. I haven't called you for that. It's for something else.' A teasing smile followed the pregnant pause before she took the next shot, 'Hope you will bend your tight waist for me, Saint Mohammed.' She had a grin Mohammed pretended to ignore, but neatly faltered in the attempt.

He was sorry for her, no doubt. Suspicion was hovering over his feelings of sympathy. She threw a casual look at the house, to ratify that she had inspected it before, and displayed an enacted worry, to prove that she had really worried earlier, about the mess it was.

'Sir and madam will come tomorrow. You have to pick them up from airport. But before that, you can see what condition the house is. It needs to be done up and I have to shift to my *chawl* before they arrive.'

Mohammed was not given much time to keep hanging his 'so what' look.

'And you have to do that.' She was pleading or ordering; Mohammed couldn't figure out. Confusion usually pops up on a face, but Mohammed's went blanker.

'Don't clinch your ass so tight. I will guide you. I can't exert much. Just tell me when you will be in mood. They will be reaching around 2 pm, tomorrow.' She came from her dick-teasing to have-to-do-it, without a break.

'I can't come tomorrow morning . . . I have so many things to do.' It simply slipped out of his mouth.

'Do it tonight then?' Her voice was firm and sincere.

Shadows of the coming events looked curious yet menacing to him. Mohammed somehow gave a nod and left to come back after wrapping up his day.

He returned at 9 pm. Mary was in better shape.

'Go and have your bath first.' She was genuine, in spite of the intended subtext.

'Bath . . . bath for what?' Mohammed's apprehension was real.

'Not to sleep with me. Don't panic. You have not seen yourself for years, it looks. I don't know how your wife allows you to touch her. Anything you try to clean will be dirtier. Everything is not a broken down car, and also if you look up, a broken down car is not everything, you moron.' She switched to her naughty self.

She took a direct shot, gazing at his frontal, 'What the hell you will clean up? First clean your own mess; you greasy guy.'

Mohammed felt more than embarrassed, and cornered too. He was standing as if asked to strip publicly.

'Leave your soiled and oiled clothes dry. I will wash them at my *chawl*. Have a clean bath and then wear the pant and shirt I have kept for you in the bathroom.' She literally pushed him.

This was unreal for Mohammed; an out of life kind of experience. A heavenly shower in a plush bathroom of a rich man; a woman who was not his talking to him when he was taking off his clothes; it was like a dream. Indistinguishable waves of fear and excitement, tickled him till he opened the shower. Mary's instructions came loud. He had never so lavishly shampooed his hair. He had a wholesome bath. Looking at nude Mohammed in life-size mirror, he was expecting Mary to cross limits of her titillating remarks. He was wrong. She was on, but matter-of-factly, to his surprise. His horny problem got a default treatment. It limped to normalcy on its own. Mary was suddenly a bodiless voice for him. It went still for some time before she threatened to come in and inspect what he was doing for so long. Her tone was quite motherly. For Mohammed, the woman was puzzling; every time drifting beyond his imagination.

Mohammed came out; re-incarnated. Clean and fresh. In a well-creased pant and shirt, he was another person.

Mary gave him a good full look. Mohammed's gaze was fixed at nowhere. There was silence of a minute.

'This dress is for you only, don't worry; I will tell sir.' To Mary, Mohammed looked like a child just getting ready to take his school bus. To Mohammed, it was just happening to him. He was in Mary's hands for the moment.

Mary gave him some chicken curry and bread to eat as they descended to the mundane. The house needed to be set into order. It was a task of hours.

Mohammed was precisely following Mary's instructions. Would stop and wait when unclear. Mary while guiding

Mohammed placidly ironed the left-over clothes. He got a few slaps on the wrist for his silly response and clumsy handling. Mary kept asking long questions about his life while his replies came in monosyllables. With a mixed feeling of sensuousness and scare, he touched many feminine articles for the first time in his life.

It was the time to go; close to mid-night. He said a curt no to Mary's offer to stay back. No time is so late in Bombay and for Mohammed it was never. Also Mohammed wished this illusory sequence to end, before it bangs into a reality this way or that way. He needed to come out and pick up the life he was living and would be living.

Suddenly Mary was in shivers. Mohammed stood still until she stretched out her hand for him to hold. Mohammed precariously helped her to be on her feet.

'Take me to bed', she murmured.

Mohammed felt there was something more than he could understand; pre-ordained or pre-planned. He felt like telling Mary—'Sorry, I am out of this. I have to go where I belong to.'

Something stopped him. That was his guilt perhaps. Mary had done so far nothing that allowed him to doubt her intentions.

He suppressed his thoughts and took Mary into the room, carefully holding her arm. He cautiously made her lie in the bed and covered her body to the chest.

He administered pills to her precisely following her instruction, till she went to sleep. Mohammed passed his night lying on the floor. Mary was better when she got up. She got dropped to her *chawl*.

The sunrise spotlighted the dress Mohammed was wearing. He thought of putting on his soiled and oiled clothes, his second skin, back. But Mary had taken it along for washing. He was not much worried how Negi and his wife would react to his audacity. They were people with a heart. Many a times they gave their old clothes for him and his family. He was worried more to think of those idle asses at Mohan Batteries who wouldn't ever miss this wonderful chance to pull his leg.

Thinking was a problem with Mohammed, moving on was not. He kicked himself to usher in. Potshots came, some failed to get registered with him and he overlooked the rest. Jokes apart, but everyone was happy for him. Around noon he told Rajesh Bajaj about his plan to pick up Negi and his wife from the airport. Bajaj was all yes; in fact, happy to hear the news.

Mohammed had never seen the airport from inside, outside was a familiar place. Waiting outside the airport and spotting his passenger dot at the exit gate was his skill.

He went ahead sheepishly to take the hand baggage from Mrs Negi as he saw them emerge. She was first taken aback to discover that the neatly dressed person, she missed out, was Mohammed. It took her a while to realize that it was her husband's dress. She was amused. How it came to Mohammed, she passed up.

'You are looking dashing Mohammed. You should always dress up like this. In fact, the size fits better on you.'

Harish Negi was not pleased to see Mohammed wearing his dress and was certainly displeased to hear the words of approval from his wife. Mohammed felt sized. He tried to diffuse the situation, 'It was Mary who insisted. I never wanted to . . .' He left his sentence half but that fully intensified the air. A silence prevailed till they reached home.

'Mary is very ill. She is at her *chawl*', He muttered as he dropped the last bag on the doorsill.

At about 8 in the evening, Mohammed got a call from Tara madam to come fast as Mary was to be taken to the hospital urgently. Mr Negi would be late from office, she explained.

Mohammed was there in no time. They went to Mary's *chawl*. Mary was looking drained and pale. She had a few vomits, the neighbours informed. Mrs Negi with the help of a neighbour made her lie on the back seat. Mrs Negi sat in the front with Mohammed, for the first time. Against his habit, and for the caution from Tara madam, he drove down smoothly to Shushrusha hospital, not far away.

Mary was taken to the Casualty for examination. Howling of pain, she repeatedly asked Tara madam to stay outside. Her pleading became vehement.

'I will be fine, madam. I beg of you, please stay outside. It is nothing, just stomach pain.' Mrs Negi felt odd and also cagey.

Mohammed was shocked. To his credulous mind it looked a case of pregnancy; Mary pregnant from Negi. Everything started falling in place for him. Seeing the patient distressed the lady doctor signalled Mrs Negi to wait outside.

After ten minutes, the whimpers stopped and the doctor came out.

'There is nothing to worry. It's a case of severe colitis. The pain was acute, so we have given her sedatives. She is sleeping now. We have put her on intravenous drugs; she will be fine in just two days. You can now go and see her.'

Tara went inside. Mary was unconscious; her limbs spread. She looked innocent and pitiable. Tara was feeling sad for her while lifting the green cloak from her chest.

Mary had tight and shapely breasts. She further removed Mary's dress first for the curiosity that turned into suspicion suddenly. Mary had clean underarms; too clean for a housemaid. Something was disturbing Tara. She wanted to see more of this housemaid. She couldn't believe Mary's skin was much silkier and smoother than hers. The thought woodened her for a while. Mary was stark naked beneath the gown. Tara looked around for Mary's undergarments. She had to push Mary aside to check under the bed sheet. A pair of olive coloured bra and panties fell down. It was velvety, new and lavish.

Tara picked the lingerie up and kept it under Mary's pillow. It was her brand, imported, available only at Customs notified shops. But the size was smaller. Harish Negi was fond of this brand and olive was his favourite colour. Tara has been wearing this brand for years and always had at least one pair of olive colour. She was full of disgust.

She came home, dazed. Asked Mohammed to wait in the car and went inside her house. With her just acquired painful still clearer vision, Tara examined her house, her eyes moving like a searchlight. She could see Mary sleeping in bed, with Harish Negi, in the night gown Negi bought her from Customs duty free shop. Her disgust for Negi was turning into anguish. She felt like torching her possessions into ashes.

She called up Harish Negi; one number and another till she got him.

'Mary is in the hospital and I am leaving for Nasik right now', she sounded metallic cold. She had not inferred anything yet her tone pulled Harish Negi up from his roots.

'But how have you decided suddenly? How will you go at this time? Just wait, I will be home in some time. We will talk.' He was fumbling.

'There is nothing left to be talked. I am not leaving you forever. I have one more Negi in my life. I would never want him to know the character of his father or he might feel inherited to do debauchery. Everything will be perhaps alright soon but I doubt anything will be same again.' And she dropped the receiver.

Mohammed drove her down to Nasik that very night. He had no clue of what was happening. He came back after two nights.

Harish Negi called up Rajesh Bajaj a few times. Tara every time kept the phone back without a hello. Rajesh Bajaj was fuming. His wicked mind couldn't rid of the sinister visuals. He was sure how a woman exacts revenge once outraged. He had sensed the tremor in Negi's house. That was Rajesh Bajaj. He didn't speak it out to anyone. His mind was brimming with envy at the moment.

He could literally see distressed Mrs Negi calling lost Mohammed to her bedroom late in the night.

'I have a severe headache. Can you just press my head a little?'

Bajaj knew how this 'a little' ends into a crazy coitus that relieves the headache of a disturbed soul. In every breath he spat an abuse on Mohammed.

Harish Negi had known Mohammed for years and had only a soiled and smelly image of him. He found it strongly superimposed with another Mohammed neatly dressed up; wearing neat and clean pants and shirt. *Mohammed dismantling Tara; fixing her lose nuts, removing the rust, cleaning her clogged jet, pouring cool water in her red hot radiator and finally fuelling her tank to get her ready for the bumpy road of life. Tara feeling her body overhauled, her soul repaired.*

Harish Negi wished he could put his hand into his head to clench out this vile imagery. His hands were numb with the guilt.

Mohammed came back the third day. Negi's house was locked. After parking the car, he came to Mohan Batteries. Rajesh Bajaj scanned him while Mohammed placed the key on the table. He didn't feel the need to say, 'Give it to Negi.'

'You mother-fucker, you think it's your father's shop. You can come anytime and go anywhere you feel like. Get lost from here; I don't want to see your face.'

Mohammed was silent and that was the only answer he had. Neither he was to go anywhere nor Bajaj had an option. He knew. Mohammed's stoic silence was only cementing the pile of lewd images Bajaj had in his mind. No one ever knew what happened between Mohammed and Tara in those two days. And nights, of course. Why Mohammed stayed there for two nights, everyone at Mohan Batteries tried to guess.

Mary's revelation began once she discovered her underwear and bra. She looked at them like the 'attire of a harlot' she would never put on again. Her subtil of heart took her away from the adultery she was in. From hospital she went straight to the church. '*And she heard a great voice out of heaven saying, Behold, the tabernacle of God is with the men . . . And he said unto him, it is done. I am Alpha and Omega, the beginning and the end. I will give unto him that is athirst of the fountain of the water of life freely.*'

She never went back to Negis' after that. Harish Negi and Tara left Bombay after some time. Bajaj told every time a new story. With the efflux, he started repeating them.

Mary brought lunch for Mohammed one day and then never stopped. Mohammed whenever got late, stayed in her *chawl* that was close by. It became more frequent with the time.

He goes for *namaz* every Friday.

One late evening while Mary and Mohammed were sitting outside her *chawl* after a tiring day, Mary asked him 'You know it was Gabriel, the messenger of God, who conveyed the message of God to Mohammed.'

'Yes', said Mohammed, 'Father Sebastian told me something like that the day I was baptised and taken into Bosco shelter. Before that, I remember they called me Mohan when I was in Dharavi. I don't remember much.'

'Mohan . . . You know Mohan was another name of Lord Krishna.'

'Yes, the whole world knows. But it's my first name I only know.'

He paused and said, 'Don't tell it to anyone, and never to Bajaj. The bastard will never let me enter his shop.'

Mary moved closer to Mohammed and pecked a kiss on his forehead.

Easy Savitri

In her imagination, Future is like yards and yards of plain-cloth, new and uncut. It has an untouched feel, and the seminal smell of starch. Present is a sewing machine that runs over the cloth, monotonously, for hours. It stitches Future into different shapes. Present sweats. The smell is peculiar, coital. Past is like wash and wear, again and again for years, and it has the smell of everything familiar.

She is now her past. She lived her future long ago; if life was a sewing centre. It wasn't, she knew well. She has lived it playing hard.

Those who thought their charm was good to sponsor their lust got caught in a tight situation. It wouldn't work with Savitri. Hard pressed to shell out twenty rupees, they came out stifled. Some had Savitri, and some kept their twenty rupees. Everybody earned the right to denounce, 'Savitri is a whore.'

There were those who desired exclusivity. Jealousy making desire wait is not unusual. But the promise of a better future was not enough to beguile Savitri. She didn't want an owner. She had seen where that comfort led. After playing all their cards, they too came away fuming. They found a stronger reason to declaim, 'Savitri is a whore of a woman.'

Let them seethe. Savitri won't oblige without her twenty bucks. Twenty rupees was something, when Savitri was not even thirty.

Now she is in the close shadow of sixty. Her face is radiant, still. It's perhaps the glow of fulfilment.

Widowhood's been a severe loss always, everywhere. Here, it was first a stigma and then a continuing torment. Living within the dotted circle of this tragedy, there were still some gritty sufferers who made their life worth living.

The realization that the most covered part of the body can actually turn the wheel of life comes when everything is gone. The insightful appreciate this art of living without a husband. The worldly wise know that not moral character, but a careful involvement with immorality is what keeps one going. They called it 'chest', meaning the heart and everything around it. If one has that one has life, vivacity. The majority whined, 'Shamelessness!'

Some of those not-so-sad widows made it better than they would have with the fucking marital bliss. Savitri is one that I know.

Prabhati was a lanky boy. His adolescent frame had showed promise of a well-built man, but asthma belied the promise. Not from nowhere; many were ready to swear that it descended straight from his father.

In the wee hours of the first night appeared the first sign. A mix of uncontrollable anger and ripping anxiety triggered the attack, and no doubt, Savitri caused it.

A commonplace virgin, Savitri had no practical experience of sex. Not that she had conscientiously saved herself for the great nuptial night. In those crowded surroundings, getting the membrane ruptured was more difficult than keeping it intact. Yet, Savitri had a good idea of the experience without ever having had it. Blame it on her mother. She too was an early widow. Fate, like a vengeful killer, hits sometimes repeatedly at the same spot.

Chasing a dream, Savitri's father went far into the eastern woods and what came back was his dead body. After deliberations, death alone was found to be its own cause. Like it is, most of the time. Her mother's hand on the sewing machine plus her widowhood made her the popular choice to run the newly established sewing centre. Those were the days of 'roti, kapda aur makaan' in India. While bread, clothing, and shelter were on man's account; cooking, sewing and upkeep were woman's burden. Sewing, next to cooking, came to be the skill a girl was required to develop before womanly contours were visible on her physical frame. It was not for nothing that girls were going out to learn sewing in droves.

A sewing centre is purely a woman's world. There, a man's existence is reduced to merely a quaint set of genitals. The self-appointed king of the universe is only a phallus here, and every mention of him provokes laughter. That's as he deserves perhaps. For a woman's divinely designed anatomy, they have no dearth of metaphors.

There was always sexual innuendo for any part or movement of the sewing machine, be it the pairing of the thread and the needle or the incessant motion of the piston or even the process of oiling the machine through its many curious and tiny holes.

A caution: linking this kinky stuff to their character is a sign of male myopia. It had more to do with an oppressive society that was tearing them apart while they playfully stitched their lives together. Savitri intently listened to every bit of this vagina chinwag. It never let her take her school-books seriously.

One day, wrapped in a wedding sari, she followed in the footsteps of Parbhati and entered his house. And then came the night she showed Parbhati what he couldn't have imagined in his wildest dreams. Parbhati was in heaven for a while. He wished he could stay there forever. But climax is the beginning of the end; and the end came, riding on a wave of disgust. He gave Savitri a kick; targeting the middle of her body in that darkness.

'Get down of my bed, you bloody whore!'

This was the first time she was labelled 'whore'. The word passed like the far-off bark of a stray dog in a winter night; heard but not registered. Finding her still crumpled up on his bed, he got up, dragged her down and kicked again.

No cry. She was waiting for the brute to stop. It would. She had heard the ghastly yet believable tales from many in the sewing centre. The act gets over, and a violent ghost appears from nowhere. Don't speak a word to it. The advice came with every recount. And so once it was over, she spread herself on the floor and went to sleep. A few kicks here and there are acceptable from eff'ing life so far the devil provides the essentials to remain on its side. Savitri was game.

Sexual gratification was not enough to soothe Parbhati's ignited mind. A part of him was awake, quarrying the past of this woman.

Sudden sounds of tortured breathing woke Savitri up. Prabhati let her massage his chest but only till he regained his breath. She was shown her place quickly after. Asthma that was knocking at the door for some time came to be reckoned that night.

A new bride was like a little known story. Those who saw it happening were usually not good at describing it. And those with a nose would hardly get a whiff. Savitri got her share of comments. Days passed. Nights too, but rarely without a ghastly hour. Brutal insemination is curiously more fructifying than pleasant sex. It was just over a month and Savitri missed her period.

Parbhati got the news through a neighbourhood harridan. While lauding Parbhati's manhood, the old woman succeeded in sowing doubt in his mind, 'Lucky Parbhati, you will be a father in just nine months. Savitri has brought luck to you. Good deal you got, my son. Now don't hit her at a wrong place, you butcher. One who boots his luck asks for ill-fortune.'

Pregnancy brought some solace in Savitri's life. Now even if agitated, Parbhati was physically restrained. When lost control, he would hit at safe spots; mostly legs. It reminded Savitri of her mother's advice, '*Aye lass*, be careful, don't lash the buffalo now. And not at all on the belly. She is carrying now. Her signs are of a female calf; one more buffalo in next three years, God willing.'

Signs Savitri showed were of a boy—*a harbinger of the clan. The fruit of one's Karma of the last birth.*

'She is light and agile. A girl would have caused sluggishness.' Grandmothers opined confidently.

Signs had misled before, but rarely. Parbhati was now kind enough to get her sweetmeats every other night. Pickles came from experienced neighbours. Life was slowly rolling on track. The moral deductions at the end of every dirty conversation at the sewing centre were not wrong. *Taming a man was a game of endurance.* Savitri saw it happening.

Asthma continued its visits; intermittently, and then frequently. Savitri would make him a concoction of cloves and black pepper before bed. Her sister-in-law would sleep with her while Parbhati slept in the cowshed. This was a way to check lapses. An aroused man is a wild animal. Her pregnancy would not be a strong enough deterrent at such times.

Winter is not on the side of an asthma-patient; every neighbour will woefully vouch for this. Asthma steals the patient's sleep and the jarring sounds of heavy breathing in those sepulchral night-hours won't let anyone within earshot sleep either. The chest needs to be kept warm to reduce the risk of attack. The hot smoke of home-made tobacco was a relief in the dew-drenched nights of a freezing winter.

Pangs around, life was, nevertheless, steady for Savitri. It's sometimes a way the devil corners its victim.

There was no income. Yet, there was money. Parbhati was sinking further into debt every day. He was pledging his ancestral land one bit after another. Five acres is a short run when one has nothing but a foolish hope of getting it released from a windfall. Savitri was uneasy. Something bad was around the corner, she felt.

It was a voice from her heart, like a look of suspicion in a child's eyes when offered more than the promise. She would hush her inner bird every time it came to squeak.

Savitri went from the glow of a would-be to the blues of an about-to-be mother, and the fateful day of labour dawned. Elderly women hung around, cheering, while the seasoned midwife dug into her stock of one-liners while setting up for the haul. 'It was you who had the fun lying down! Remember your mother now. You have squeezed a stout man into a skeleton, now give him a lovely boy.' She pulled the slimy lump out with a heave; head first.

Even before it was fully out, she knew it was a girl. A mild cry sounded. The news was out. Parbhati has a daughter.

The gloom was not of a daughter's birth but of the death of a son that was expected. There was no reward for the midwife, so she had to scamper away, immediately after howsoever uncaringly she finished her basic job.

Preparations were abandoned half way. Savitri would eat just hot porrridge for a few days before returning to her regular meals; no special recipes for her. And no postpartum luxury. The confinement would be cut short and she would be back to work within a week. The new-born and her mother will face a deadening neglect. Nonstop barbs from the corner Parbhati's ailing mother was lying were boding. Life was set to come back in a more merciless version. Savitri knew.

Parbhati's silence broke like an iron nail pierces a bare foot. One realizes only after it's almost an inch inside the flesh. He slapped her with a suddenness that made her ears ring. 'You bitch, where have you brought this s in from, to put in my lap?'

It took a while for Savitri to grasp the import of what he said. Her gaze went up for the first time and got fixed into Parbhati's eyes. It just happened, she had no intent. She had never imagined this moment would come one day. She couldn't take her stare away.

It was as if a statue you passed every day, one day lifted its eye-lids, looked straight into your eyes and then turned stone-still again. It will not blink now. You are asked to choose. You might be the king of your universe; you will still be shaken for a moment. But since you are the king of your universe, your choices are unlimited. You choose to quell the revolt. Parbhati turned into a four-armed fury. Savitri was a daruma doll that fell every time it was hit, then got up and stared back into his eyes.

Something in her was rising for the first time to fight and overcome her misfortune.

It was dusk. She didn't try to overcome her feeling to not have her meal. 'Never turn your anger on your food,' the echo of her mother's counsel went unheard. Now it was her turn to sleep in the cowshed with her newborn. Her sister-in-law went to sleep beside her mother.

Parbahti took charge of his regular bed; the biggest item he got in dowry. It was a fine setting for the next act. And the opening was horrifying. When Parbhati didn't come out of his room past 7 in the morning, the sister-in-law went in to check. He was lying as if thrown away in a storm; legs dangling over the bed like the half-broken branches of a tree. His eyes were open, pupils still. His body was cold.

Neighbours recalled the sounds of heavy breathing they had heard past midnight. Some said it was quiet after the three stars crossed Gurdaram's mansion. That would be around 3am on a long winter night.

Asthma finally took Parbhati's life away, was the general opinion. He was sent to the other world with all the proper rituals. A close relative did the formalities for the male survivor in the family. Gurdaram didn't allow anyone to spend a penny. That finally made up an amount, in Gurdaram's calculation, that put all the five pledged acres, safely out of reach of any of Parbhati's survivors to reclaim.

Before people returned from the cremation, the rumour was out. 'It's handiwork.'

He had beaten up Savitri last evening, everyone knew. She did or it happened—'The *dayan* has swallowed her husband' was the irrefutable conclusion. Parbhati's mother put her stamp on it.

Gurdaram bore the burden of running late Parbhati's household for a couple of months, and then one day sent a message. It was for Savitri to come and check the account. She was now the head of the family. His stance was, 'I can't afford to have a blemish on my white robe. I have also to go to His house one day. She better take this account-sheet and check for herself. My house is always open to her but the account should be kept clean. My father—God give him a place in heaven—always taught me fair dealing.'

She held the paper as if it had her fate written on it. She felt a chill down her spine. Gurdaram's face was calm; unreadable. She gathered herself, 'The paper is fine, Owner; I know you will not be unfair to a helpless widow. But my point is a job; I need some work to run my house. I have to earn now, you know.'

Gurdaram turned softer, 'That will also happen; don't worry. The one who gives the beak also gives the feed. Let some time pass.'

He pushed a few currency notes into her hand with a postscript, 'The undemanding give-and-take I had with Parbhati I will continue with you too. I will never turn my back on a needy widow.'

After having touched rock bottom, life was to lift off into a different direction. Savitri had no clue. Life seemed to her like the train journey she had had once—only once. A new world comes at you at high speed and flies past without staying for a moment.

She started working as a mason's help. Her job was to bring water from the pond, mix it with the mud to make daub, fill it up in a cast-iron salver and then pass it on to the bricklayer. For hours, for days. At ten rupees a day. Saving twenty thousand would take more than a lifetime. She knew, even with her uneducated calculation. She had to repay Gurdaram twenty thousand rupees. Bringing up her daughter and feeding Parbhati's old mother was an extended part of her own existence.

She realised the meaning of sympathetic lines people crossed while passing by. Her work had brought her to a level that allowed some liberty with the veil. She would nonchalantly cover her face to avoid piercing glances from sunken eyes struggling to figure out the naked female face. Her eyes would now meet many eyes that had a single intention.

One day Savitri learned through an oblique remark that she was available. She didn't know who made this announcement on her behalf. She also learnt soon enough, that Savitri was ready to do anything for money. Anything was not as general as it sounds; it was pretty specific—*she is ready to loosen the garter.*

She didn't mind it too much. She looked within herself and honestly came to the conclusion, 'Yes, I am ready for a quick fix, if it could make some money for me.'

She had to save twenty thousand to reclaim the five acres from Gurdaram.

I heard a lot of stories about her. 'Savitri could sort out five men in a day. She had the skill to finish the job in five minutes!'

Days went like sparrows pick up grains.

From nowhere came the boon of Emergency. India was another country overnight. She went to the hospital, like people go to a fair; happy and excited for her hysterectomy. She got compensation of two hundred rupees and some beneficial contacts in the town.

After it was open to all, Gurdaram also made some advances, but was refused. Agitated, he made a blunt offer of double the amount; not cash, mind you, but to be adjusted in her account.

'No Owner, no adjustment with you; and no lying down under your sinful weight. I am a chaste woman. No man has really been able to have me yet.' She was full of vitriol.

'You bloody whore, don't give me that talk. I know your character. You sleep with anyone for twenty bucks!'

She was in giggles to see him fuming.

But that was not true. There was one Ladha, the vegetable vendor. She would sleep with him without the twenty bucks. In Ladha's small cottage, I heard so many things about Savitri. In our house, no would talk about her; and certainly not when there was a man around. Savitri would never enter our courtyard. She would pass coyly by, head covered like a new bride.

I saw her face for the first time while she was at her teasing best with Ladha. She knew me so well, I never thought. It's a strange feeling to meet face-to-face a person you have seen for years in veil. The veil makes life a one-way show.

She shot an overtly double meaning teaser to Ladha, 'Your brinzals stale fast, you should keep them sprinkled.'

His retort was, 'It's good enough for you.'

'For me?' She made a quick return with a few loud clicks of her tongue, 'You don't know my taste. I like something fresh, as fresh as a bunch of grapes.' And gestured to me through slit-eyes.

Ladha was amused. He was not jealous.

The 'bunch of grapes' was beyond my thoughts. It was a painter's imagination. I was amazed to hear it from Savitri.

'So you want a taste of this young boy.' Ladha laughed out loud like a child. I was ill at ease.

'He's of my Pankhuri's age; maybe a little older. He looks like a raw mango; I am salivating to bite one.' She kept gazing straight at me. I was pink with embarrassment.

While scurrying away, she looked back at me with a scrutiny in her eyes.

Pankhuri was Savitri's daughter. The name Pankhuri was again a coinage of sewing centre. She first heard the word there and it stayed with her. Every pregnant woman at the centre prayed for the reward of conjugation—a boy. Fruit was a metaphor for a boy. A girl was *pankhuri*—a petal. Women at the sewing centre always preened about their vaginal petals but when it came to delivering, they craved for a 'fruit' always.

Savitri was not sad to have given birth to a girl. She was happy; it was her first child. She had always dreamed of having a home full of children. She would have her fruit, she was sure. Until her wish was cut short. She named her daughter Pankhuri. While giving her bath, she would wash her petals concernedly, and fondly.

Panhkuri was 15 one day; talkative and charming. Open hearted like her mother. I always found her looking at me. Adoration spilling from her eyes. She would press close to me whenever she got a chance. I was good-looking, with an education; a poor girl's vision of prince charming.

I met her usually at crowded functions. Our bodies would try to cross boundaries to get twined. We met in the dark to feel each other more closely. Guilt was mostly mine as I only made the overtures. She was always restrained. Getting physical is the last thing for a female. For a male, it's first. For her it was stealing flowers to offer to her deity, nothing sinful. For me it was snatching a few from her basket to smell and throw away; disgusting.

It was soon over—I left my village to go to college. From there I went straight to my job at a daily paper. I would only return to the village when I could manage leave for a day or two.

Savitri had finally taken back her five acres from Gurdaram. Repaid every penny she owed. She never questioned the atrocious rate of interest. She had lost that chance when she refused to lie with the usurper.

She married off her daughter to a good-looking teacher—so what if he was a widower? He was tall and healthy. His first wife had died just six months after the marriage. And if that was not so, why then would he marry the daughter of an ill-reputed woman? There was another reason, as the worldly-wise knew—the five acres of land. Whatever it was, Pankhuri was happy and Savitri was relaxed.

She could now spend most of her time helping others. Once considered morally deficient, Savitri was now socially in demand. When no man was around, she would slip into our courtyard, if only to deliver a few quick respectful massage-strokes on the forelegs of elderly women basking in the sun. She always liked to spend a few moments asking after the well-being of these supposedly single-man women.

Whenever she saw me, she would come and put her hand on my head.

There came a time she qualified to be called old.

I could never forget Savitri. Whenever I began to write a story, she would come to mind.

Like she was teasing me—'Think of me if you want to write about something really interesting.'

Each time I would pass, not having the courage to take her on. I don't know what was stopping me.

The day came when I decided to begin her story and then I had to stop halfway. To complete it, I strongly felt that I had to know one thing for sure—the truth about how Parbhati died. Did Savitri truly kill her husband or was it just rumour? It was my story, I could have twisted it whichever way I wanted, you would think. But no, it's not so; you can't do that. A story has to be true, however much fiction you might add to it. I had to know the truth.

The last time when I was in my village I finally got my chance. After paying her respects to my mother she came inside looking for me. She asked after me kindly.

I gathered my courage. 'I have written a story about you Savitri-aunty.'

She was greatly amused. 'A story about me? You must be joking, my son. What's there to write about me—a poor, illiterate and base woman? You should write a story about yourself. We saw you running around naked in these streets and you are today a well-known person. We see your name in the newspapers.'

'That's not a story, Savitri-aunty. There has to be something interesting and mysterious about a person to become a story. And you have that.'

She was flattered, but casual still.

'Your choice, son! Write the story of this characterless woman. People will read and ridicule Savitri; a woman of low virtue. There was that sati Savitri who brought her husband back from the God of death and here's me, the sinner.' She laughed with a tinge of pain. She readied to leave.

'But I can't complete the story till I know the truth of . . .' I paused to assess her reaction, 'Your husband's death. Did you kill him or did he die of his illness?' I asked almost in panic.

'Oh!' Then after a long pause, 'You can't write your story without knowing that?' She wasn't expecting this from me, I guessed.

Unnerved, I offered an explanation. 'It's not that I am going to write down what really happened. Knowing will only help me to write the story better.'

'I will help you, my son.' She sounded cold and firm, and was quiet for a while.

When she spoke again her tone had changed, 'No, I didn't kill him. I helped him die. He asked for death. If he had lived, I and my Pankhuri were to die. I chose what I thought was right. I don't mind even if you write this. The whole world wants to know this truth.' She walked off.

She was offended I didn't know. But she was resolute I could see.

The next day we were to return to the city. My wife was busy packing our meal for the journey while my mother played the friendly supervisor.

She is too old, my mother, and takes time to recognize a person standing right in front of her.

It was Savitri with a thin, shy boy.

'My grandson', Savitri spoke loudly for my mother's benefit. 'Pankhuri's elder son, very intelligent, just like your son was. He is the topper at his school; like your son was. He will be going to college now. Come Jeet, take Grandma's blessings.'

She brought him closer to my mother. 'Look, he's exactly like how your son looked when he was in school!'

My mother blessed the boy, and to cut Savitri, markedly ignored the gush of unsolicited comparison.

While watching these silent frames through my window, I felt an unknown dread clutch at my chest.

Savitri quickly began rubbing my mother's forelegs dangling over the cot. This was to convey, 'Keep your angst with you, old woman. If you don't want to talk I don't have time either. Fling your muffled blessings at us and I'll be on my way.'

Savitri brought the boy inside the house. Her footsteps showed purpose. Her grin was unreadable.

'My grandson, I want him to be someone like you. He will be one day, I'm sure.' And then to the boy, 'Jeet, go home now. I will come in five minutes.' The boy had been waiting for the signal and bolted.

'He looks like you, no?' Her gaze turned towards me, sarcasm in it, even as a broad smile stretched her lips.

I felt weak-kneed, suddenly. My blood seemed to freeze.

'I thought you were only friends with my Pankhuri. Still, I asked your mother to warn you. Thinking you were a nice boy. I only realized the blow when I learned that Pankhuri was pregnant. It was too late. You had gone. I had to marry her off immediately. God bless the widower teacher. He came like an angel from nowhere. My Pankhuri was lucky to escape ignominy.' She spoke breathlessly, in a low husky tone. 'And she got her Jeet.'

She continued after a pause, 'Now son, you have a story about yourself interesting—with mystery, and also with some sin, if you'd like to write it, no?

She was gone before I came out of my daze.

My mother's annoyance was obvious, 'What was that bitch whispering in your ear for so long? Now get ready. You have to go. You keep on doing favours to these ungrateful people and they keep chasing you like beggars.'

I was not sure she remembered the day she had reprimanded me. Her words reverberated in my head. 'If I hear something like this again, I will never forgive you. Thank God, she has not told it to your father; he would have beaten you to death otherwise!' I had been stunned by her words.

The scene was vivid in my memory. What I had done with Pankhuri, it was against her wishes, I knew. I know. And I would never forget. She had been in awe of me, and couldn't refuse.

It was set aside as a boy's misdemeanour, not a man's sin. I got away with a minor punishment. That's what I had believed so far. That the past would rise up to haunt me like this, one day, I'd never imagined.

I saw Savitri again when I was leaving. She came close. Her hand was on my head when she said, 'No hard feelings son, I got my *fruit* finally. I am happy. God bless you.'

It was by far the most difficult moment of my life. But Savitri was easy. Easy as ever.

INVISIBLE RENDITION /
MOONLIGHT MOSEY

Firmly holding his bamboo stick, gawkily he walks to the east. It's a dead summer night. No one saw him changing the route of his regular moonlight mosey. Awfully slow and wobbly, he still has a streak of steadiness. That shows his resolve. He remembers the holy city, a gateway to the upper world, is about fifty miles east of his village. His memory is no more trustworthy he knows. Pictures suddenly go blank, words get lost, names are erased as he attempts to take a dip in his past; a span of just 37 years. He is drifting out of this world.

'I have to keep walking till the earth ends,' he reminds himself.

He is not desperate. He is not depressed. He is clear. He makes some weird movements and smiles as his shadow imitates him.

'I can't get rid of this damn thing,' he mumbles.

He looks at his shadow following him. He feels the damn thing is chasing him out of life.

One who enjoys less suffers lesser. Maru is a testimony in flesh. The problem is with his bones, and the germ lies deep into his genes. To him, it's just a game the fate one day decided to play with him.

Maru has *ankylosing spondylitis*. Like most of his folks, he cottons it on as *bamboo-spine*. It came from nowhere, 18 years back. When his doctor told some more outlandish names of his ailment, Maru had no choice than to duck the spray. In his guess, the names were of unlucky people who were the first known victims of the malady that singles him out today. How unfortunate it would be to become famous thanks to the disease one suffers from. It was dismaying. He sympathized with them until realized that these were the highly educated guys who fathomed out hitherto unknown facts about this godforsaken ailment. Awe replaced sympathy. Maru was never more scared of anything than books and school.

It knocked from inside. Naively, he took it an ordinary twitch in his neck. A recurrent problem with two-legged beasts of the burden. Maru was one. He would put his neck, and if not sufficient his back too, to shift any weight only because, if not he, someone else would do it. That was 18 years ago when he was barely nineteen, stout and muscular.

He tried all those usual neck-setting tricks he could do himself, and with the help of others. There was a moment of relief. Elusive but it was. The trouble would hide for a while only to poke back. He went for massage of one kind and the other, from self-proclaimed healers debatably one better than the other. The result was a slightly longer respite. Nothing more. The gremlin stayed around. It got confirmed as the re-appearances came to be more and more retributive.

It is a ghost—opinion emerged. Consensus followed.

Alas! Maru's mother is not there. She would have made the demon's life miserable had she not died in a dastardly attack of one such rogue of a soul two years ago. Everyone bemoaned. A ghost pushed her down in her sleep from the roof with no parapet, only to be discovered dead next morning. She was on the hit-list of the ghost community for quite some time. *Everyone knew.* For nothing but her relentless fight against the evil spirits. She knew the antidotes, one more intricate and powerful than the other to make the toughest of the rascals run for his life. *People had seen ghosts begging for her mercy.* She would let the culprit off the hook only after revealing who he was, and not before publicly swearing that it would never cross the fence again.

He never talked about it, but Maru resented the hush talk about his mother's link-up with evil spirits. Her crusade for common good earned her a status, and also bought Maru's silent vote. Her untimely death gave her a straight entry into the community of spirits, many believed. She was now a gentle ghost, several would testify by recounting friendly encounters they had with her and the unanticipated favour they got to come alive and narrate.

Maru had never faced a ghost. Nor ever he tried to peep into the shadowy world his mother almost governed. For some reason, she chose to keep him away from these dark alleys. But the ghostly trappings suddenly changed his mind. He now desired to know about ghosts. *If my mother is a ghost, sooner or later she will get me out of the clutches of this rascal sitting on my neck.* The thought made him feel shielded.

He often saw in his dreams—'*his mother is sitting like a queen amongst the obedient ghosts. He shouts to tell her how one of her scoundrels was tormenting her loved son. Words don't come out of his throat. He cries in frustration, and tries harder to get his mother's attention*'. A streak of pain would rise in his neck, waking him up. He hoped to succeed one day to let his mother know about his woe.

Till that happens, he knew, he would have to walk miles to find someone capable of checking the damage. Complete riddance is going to be a longer haul he suspected. Still tried every suggestion that came. Maru was a mountain of patience. More arduous the exorcising ritual more it was convincing. The thought—'there is no escape'—never crossed his credulous mind.

Futility brings fatigue, and it did. Prescription from the local quacks lost the draw slowly. He couldn't finally save his neck from lending into the hands of a qualified specialist in spite of strong resistance from many of his well-wishers. The argument was—'these doctors can do nothing much in such reprisals of fate. These incurable ills come only to make doctors realize that there is someone sitting right up.' Examples were cited where desperate doctors irreparably spoiled the case. And then death had to reluctantly intervene to cut the ordeal short. Rarely, with an extreme stroke of luck, one stumbled on to some good spiritual healer before the countdown of breaths came to a naught.

Maru had to face not so many questions and just a couple of tests. That's all, and the result came. The doctor concluded—'You are suffering from a rare kind of spondylitis.' The full import of the sad news was delivered in instalments with the bottom-line remaining intact every time—*there is no treatment. Poor Maru would have to live with it till his last breath.* The best, *meaning the only,* way was to take up some regular exercises to keep the body mobile and some medicines to kill the pain when unbearable.

The obvious ease and the inadequacy of efforts on the part of the doctor didn't go down well with Maru. His discontent was subscribed by many of his folks. *These doctors don't know nothing.* It was now the turn of some philosophical view and it came without delay. *'Nature reserves the remedy of the biggest problem it throws at us. The caveat is that she never allows anything to happen before its time.'*

The matter thus landed into the *very long hands of time* whereas in a short span Maru's condition went from bad to worse. He accepted it as a game between him and his fate and got ready to play as good as he could. Strikingly awkward it looked but Maru kept walking. Women and kids stopped and watched him walk till gone out of sight. His face was not his. He was no more the Maru village knew.

His condition reached what doctor simplified as bamboo spine. The word bamboo cleared to him and to his folks many things about this complex malady. They now know that Maru's spine has become one-piece rod, like a bamboo. His many years old x-ray clearly shows a straight bamboo stick with no joints. It has very faint markings where vertebrae have fused into adjoining ones. That's evident from Maru's peculiar walk. Now, the village has not just clarity but also a simple name—*rear-bamboo*—for this creepy illness.

Walking looks like a huge struggle, still he does it with a spirit of comeback. That has perhaps saved him from worse. Time has given a bamboo also in his hand to balance the wobbliness caused by the one in his back. His love for physical work is still alive. He helplessly gazes at people working, from the sidelines like an untimely retired sportsman. The difference is that he hardly pokes his nose or even passes a comment how others should do their work.

He loved work like an ant does but always had an aversion to talk about it. He never had the urge to speak about the work he finished or the one that was pending; uncharacteristic of work enthusiasts. He just kept moving from one task to another, without much of planning. Body is for work, rest is necessary but only to get ready for the next job. That was Maru's purpose of life. His conduct was a testimony.

Maru hated school as much as he loved toiling. His mother made a few attempts to initiate him into studies against his reluctance. She was soon convinced by the teachers and fortune-tellers that Maru had little chance of success in that direction. Maru welcomed the verdict and the mother had to put a seal of acceptance without much of whinge, no doubt, with a scratch of pang.

Teachers could never make Maru open his mouth even by extending the liberty to go wrong. He found their charity a honey trap. Once got into that question-answer game, he would never be able to wriggle out. The alert came from within. Some declared him an imbecile and others a two-legged mule. No issue, till it saved him from the haunt the school offered.

Work was his play right since childhood. Playing with friends demanded too much of verbal interaction—he always loathed. He was a weakling but by preteens showed good signs of a tall and well-built man in making. And the sign didn't turn out false.

Strong physique and innate will to work made him the most sought after boy for all the day-to-day jobs. The closure of education window opened many of manual skills. The range was wide. From a dangerous challenge of taming an agitated bull to opening a lock of the most trusted make—he would accomplish all with same ease, and without a flaunt. He would vanish as soon as the task was over, leaving the bunch of spectators to do the talking.

Maru had sex when he was fifteen—and not that fidgety type novices get to wade through before experiencing the real. Not all-inclusive but, yes, it was explicitly sex. Incidentally it came. The woman had done some spadework probably. His skill of a locksmith got him one afternoon straight into the expert hands of a mother of two kids. In the darkish inner room while holding the lantern to show him the key-hole she kept moving closer as Maru tried one key after the other. With every attempt he felt the pressure of her breasts on his back. In that darkness it was not so cumbersome for Maru to deal with the crawly movement between his thighs; dodgy, in his second thought. She was a motherly figure for his raw feelings, he cringed. Suddenly there was a compelling silence to pilot the inevitable. The final rotation that opened the lock brought the moment of crash.

He felt her hand on the cramped little reptile seething in his pyjamas, struggling to raise the hood. He looked into her eyes. For the first time he was able to register the meaning of earnest invitation he had seen many a times.

In a few moments she was on her back holding him between her corpulent thighs. Maru found himself on a rock in the sea; afraid of the depth. In no time, she unclothed the just essential. Maru was in trance while she caught hold of the furious serpent by neck with the dexterity of a seasoned charmer and showed it the way. His body and mind maintained a discipline in spite of an urge to ravish. Everything was where it belonged to; no ransacking of body and no ravaging of soul. Maru sincerely followed the guidance from her, and made no overtures. Not his wont. Next five minutes were only of action, no sounds of ecstasy and no mumbles of compliments. She wiped him off with her petticoat the moment it got over. Life was back to the path. He gave her the key and went over to the path he came from.

Maru remained the man he was, to her, and to the world. Nothing changed. He had neither the feeling of exuberance nor of remorse. It was just another job he should be performing whenever invited to.

Men mostly have sex devoid of a pure reason. This makes women scared. Animal are better off. They never carry the baggage of memories. They never commit sins. They don't suffer the loss of virginity. They never rape. They never black mail. Maru was as simple a man as an animal.

This extraordinariness of him brought rivulets of sex in his life, from all over. The look he captured that day in the eyes of that mother of two kids was his invitation card. A young man who could never look straight into the eyes of a woman was suddenly a singular bull destined to mate a number of cows in heat. No one in the village could see this subterranean animal kingdom of chaste sex that came into existence in an over-world of sullied relationships.

Maru was a safe asylum. For the women who wished to run away from the sufferance but couldn't. Maru was a sanctuary to have freedom and happiness of few moments. The urge of revenge deeply hidden in those feminine chests would erupt finding Maru alone. At times, he would know from the glint in their eyes that the beast is away, and there's a room in his cage. It was like celebration of the freedom that never really comes.

Come, follow the undulation of my hips. And he would. Without any formal conversation, without any prelude, and without any fore play, they would get into the act. More they got beaten from their tyrant husbands more they felt the urge to desecrate the wife in them. From someone as insignificant as they were; from someone opposite to the beast they were suffering. From someone innocuous and animal-like. Maru was that perfect someone. Sex with Maru was like the fruit of liberty without the liberty. Maru wouldn't know what he was into. Nor he had a clue how it was silently spreading like an underground movement, without a tremor on the surface. The moment he saw that discrete look in those shy eyes he would know it was going to happen, now or later.

Sex with Maru was neither an act of indulgence nor of treachery. It was just sex, something very natural between a male and a female when they had to have it.

Maru's mother wished to see him married before she breathed last. One who broached the point of Maru's marriage would get a hot glass of milk in compliment. But that was not to be. She went away without giving ample notice-time to her well-wishers. Maru was left alone in the world. He was sad, not dejectedly but detachedly.

After his debut in that dim-light, the mourning month was the longest period he kept himself away from sex. When told by wisely neighbours—no work for a month, he knew sex was also out. For him, sex was not something distinctively different from work. He found both blissfully enjoyable—the difference was a few degrees of pleasure.

He hardly went out of his house during the mourning period and those discrete eye-contacts were also out of his line. Still before the month was over, it happened, unexpectedly. He didn't know it was a sin or not.

From the hue and cry outside, he could make out his cruel neighbour was again out to show his 'manhood'. The drunkard did it often but rarely to this extreme. He dragged his wife out on the street and beat her black and blue in front of everyone. Only after a serious intervention she was left howling in the lane while he dashed away in a huff. Everyone knew that he would now have a good reason to drink and not return home till next day. The woman suddenly got up and scurried back into her house to hide from darts of hurtful sympathies. Whispers filled the air for a while but with the support of surging darkness, silence enveloped the street.

It was nothing new. People had no compelling reason to get bothered. Why was she beaten was no one's concern. Compassion came to be replaced by casualness; with the frequency of the incident. What happened today was a more dramatic version of what went every other day in this or the other lane. In such a milieu no one would be bothered to care—*'what if she commits suicide'.* But Maru did. The thought crossed his mind casually first and then came back to peep in, seeing some lights blinking deep inside the dark cerebrum. She had taken a couple of times Maru over her to take a revenge on her bestial husband. Maru had no mind to figure out what really made him think of her so sympathetically. It was the empathy in his heart or the tease in his groins. He had no clue. Idleness makes a hardworking person unfamiliar to himself. Maru never took himself so serious. There was no room for self-indulgence in his uncomplicated mind. He sincerely wished that she had at least some food before she sleeps. A good sleep partly wipes off a bad day from memory. Maru kept quelling the thought propping up incessantly—*'she has committed suicide'. To settle score with her husband? To end her misery? In a fit of anger?*

The crowd will be back tomorrow morning to witness the Act two of the tragedy, if it takes place.

He remembered how easily, once following the discrete look in her eyes, he had opened her doorchain by smoothly inserting his forearm into the gap. That was also on a late night; almost this time only. He felt he won't be able to sleep without assuring himself that she was fine. *Alive.*

He went with a bowl of sweets made on the 12th day of his mother.

As he crossed the courtyard, he saw her lying on the ground. She was a bundle of rags. Intermittent sobs and shivers were the signs of life. He was pained. Her whimpers turned louder. She had perhaps seen him watching her. She started crying like a baby as he touched her. In the moon light he saw her swollen lips and lumps on her face, as she lifted it. She cried loud once and frantically swirled her head. To hint, '*no, not only this; I am hurt everywhere.*' She pulled out his hand and led it to all the points on her body she was hurt. She drove his hand on her back that had bruise marks of a stick, and to her legs to feel the blood clots and spots of skin peeled off. She then guided his hand on to her head to show a swelling as big as a potato. She was in sobs all the while. Agitatedly, she pulled him down to the cot. Suddenly she shoved her face into his lap and cried like a helpless child. He had never played elder to anyone. A woman many years elder to him nestling in his lap gave him a strange feeling. He kept patting her head believing it was giving her relief. She tightly gripped his stout waist as if saving herself from drowning in the grief. His melancholy came to surround him. It had the sad emptiness of his mother's assimilation into the elemental universe. There was a match. Intriguingly, it was a setting for sex. Becoming or unbecoming, he was not conscious of. A pained mind that apparently denies sex furtively longs for it. Sex's alleviating. She felt on her cheek the desire bulging between his thighs. She rolled her face over it, gave it the warmth of her breaths and got it ready to pierce through her grief laid bare.

To Maru's surprise, she suddenly turned wild. He had no clue that the scene of her husband thrashing her came alive in her thoughts. In a fit of fury and revenge she took off and threw her clothes aside. She was naked, stark. Maru saw a fully nude woman for the first time. With no clothes on her body, she looked like an attractive but lethal parcel of strength and aggression. She was no more a fragile and helpless creature. In a naked world, woman is perhaps stronger than man. As she tried to take his shirt off, Maru caught her labour-toned hands. He had been never without clothes in front of a woman. In that playful scuffle, she broke the garter of his pyjamas. She was in a dying hurry to get him into her.

As Maru started it in a gentle way she yelled, 'No! Don't be so nice. Hit as hard as you can, Maru! I want revenge. I have taken enough of this.' There was a cry in her voice. Maru was puzzled. He went into acceleration while she kept him prompting, frenziedly.

'That's not enough, still harder. Lynch it. Crush it. This is the only thing in my body the rascal feels is his. He comes to me only for this.'

Maru knew what she meant still her outburst left him stunned.

First time a woman was continuously burbling while Maru was at his work. He felt scared for a while but the sense of fear enhanced the excitement. It went longer than usual. Her voice died down slowly. She was tired and exhausted. Maru got up, collected her clothes and kept in her lap. In that moonlit night he could see a smile on her face. While leaving, he gave her the bowl of sweets he had brought with him. He smiled back while managing to tie up his pyjamas. While leaving, he felt an eerie presence of his mother somewhere in that full moon night.

Maru tried to fathom his soul to find if there was something wrong in what he did. He found no guilt. After a month of mourning, life came back to its original track—more and more of work, more and more of women.

Maru never felt he should get married. It is the sense of being incomplete and empty that makes one crave for a partner, for a soul-mate. Maru was complete and full in his existence; howsoever small it was.

And then came the day he felt stiffness in his neck; the ghost struck. He didn't take it seriously. The poor guy had no clue that his life was set to change forever.

His memory has gone faint, but Maru vividly remembers that moment. His last encounter with a woman was something he had not imagined in his most distant dream. The episode is still live in his memory. It came right when he was wrestling with the ghost sitting on his neck. He noticed the same discrete look of invitation in her eyes; folks longed for a passing glance of the enigmatic and beautiful face. She was the wife of the richest and the most powerful person, the landlord of the village. His three-storey mansion and its decor was often a subject-matter of gossipers. Some had partly seen its lavishness while others had only imagination. No one had an idea of the innermost part where the landlord's wife passed most of her time with part-time maids amongst other items of luxury.

He didn't believe it first. '*You have read it wrong*'— he kept snapping himself. Landlord was a tall and handsome person. Landlord's love for his wife was nothing short of infatuation, everyone knew. He adored her like a queen. There was no reason for her to home in on Maru; a man not even in her count. He tried to shoo the thought away but the look he saw in her eyes was troubling him like a hovering wasp. For days.

The verdict came one day.

Maru was called to set the mosquito net on scores of windows and ventilators of the huge mansion. He was told to get his tools along. He knew it was a job of one full day, perhaps two. It had a link to the look he saw in those two deep eyes or not, the thought bemused him. After the harvest flies would invade the village but this was the first time Maru was summoned to fix mosquito nets.

He was there in ten minutes of the call. He mind was never so muddled in life. The chaos within mounted as he saw the landlord at the gate. With the curtness he got to know his task, his clutter was suddenly over. He had gone too far in a sway, he realized. It was the landlord who called him and the job was to be done in his supervision. Maru saw no chance of getting a second reading of that look. Without a second thought he got on to the job.

The landlord was not a harsh person. He was precise and authoritative.

Maru finished half of his work by the afternoon. As he began to wind up for the lunch break, he saw a worker barging in. He was panting. Urgency was written on his face. The landlord took him aside for a quick download of the problem the poor guy was laboriously holding up. The whispers gave out that all the trucks of wheat were intercepted by the octroi inspectors, before reaching the grain market. The landlord instantly knew it was the flying squad, and not the regular guy on the check-post. There is nothing that can't be managed with the department of octroi in a state where the word octroi is synonymous to bribe. The point is that one has to take command of the situation physically to manipulate the situation. It would need some bundles of cash, no doubt.

The landlord rushed to the second story to arm himself for the encounter. The worker was rushed to call one of the part time servants. Maru, without any effort, was getting story behind the sudden frenzy from the bits and pieces he heard. It was the benefit of having an image of a non-existent being. He felt literally like a vagina that remains invisible even if the woman undresses herself fully.

The maid came running. The landlord had put on his shoes and was ready to move out. Maru kept his tools aside and went in a corner to wash his hands. When he came back, the landlord was gone and the maid was waiting to cross looks with Maru, before turning back upstairs. It was a meaningful look, a straight continuation of the smile of the moonlit night. It was not in Maru's character to enjoy such references, barely for fun. He ignored her. She didn't give up.

'The master has called me to give you the company, madam, or to guard you?' She spoke quite loud. That showed she enjoyed some liberty with the landlord's wife. Proximity between two women overrides boundaries of status. They are equal when it comes to feminine intimacy. Men are never so uncomplicated.

Her intended loud tone was an invitation for Maru to join as a silent participant.

The reply came at the same volume, 'Tell Maru to not go away for lunch. It will take a lot of time. He can eat something here only otherwise this work will take a full week to finish.'

The servant knew Maru had heard it. Maru had almost stepped out. If he wished he could go. But the voice put brakes on his feet. He had heard the lady so clearly for the first time. He stood still for a while. Then came back and opened his pack of tools to restart the work.

'Don't open that. Come up fast. Madam is calling you.' Her smile was now more emphatic. She called up through the terrace grill. Maru obeyed.

While slowly moving up the stairs he heard—'You take your heart out from your chest and hand that over to the man he won't still stop suspecting you. The man you always sleep with always thinks that given a chance you will not mind sleeping with another man. For man, woman is a curvaceous edifice around a potential cavity he pejoratively calls cunt.'

Her voice had clarity and certainty. Her last word made Maru feel like a ghost. He walked like one without making any sound of his steps. A woman speaking the word 'cunt' without caring that a man would be overhearing, made him evaporate in thin air. The two women were not even a little perturbed to know that Maru had heard what they just spoke.

'I think if you stay here with me, we will together insult womanhood', the lady asserted.

Maru realized that, in spite of a dirty touch, the language of the lady had scent of knowledge. The maid understood and went out slowly. Maru was anticipating a pregnant smile. But no, he was mistaken. She, quietly and thoughtfully, walked out of the huge and silent mansion.

The lady broke the stillness of atmosphere and brought a jug to pour water for Maru's hand wash. There was a mat and a carved silver plate with a few chosen items in it. Maru was surprised to see that the food was precisely what Maru had weakness for—crushed sugar mixed with plenty of lard, a bowl of traditional curry, a big glass of milk and salad.

He entered cautiously. It was a big hallway. There were paintings on all sides. Mystical figures of men, women, animals, and trees overlapping. It was exotic for a simpleton like him. On one side he saw a huge rack, full of books. Maru had never seen so many books at one place. He felt dizzy, overawed to think that the woman was reading so much. He felt sorry for mistaking the look in her eyes a sexual invitation. Without any words and without even looking up even once he hurriedly finished his meal. He was in an unfamiliar world and wanted go out as quickly as possible. To think about it, and to perceive it, he needed to go out of it. They lady went into an adjoining dark room and didn't come out; probably on to her afternoon siesta. That was nothing unusual of the rich particularly while treating an insignificant person. Maru took no offence.

As he was about to get up, he heard from the inner room—'Maru, just come inside once your meal is over'. Maru went numb, not able to imagine what it was for. Her tone was metallic and attitude no non-sense.

Maru could see only darkness as he stepped in.

'Come this way.'

As he turned to the voice, he saw the figure clad in white, sitting on a bed. With his dilated pupils he could barely see the outlines of the things in the room. There was something mesmerising in her voice. Cautious of his steps, he slowly went towards her.

She didn't ask him to sit, and began, 'I love my husband and he too cares a lot about me. I don't have any intention to betray him. I find it my duty to see him happy. We are married for seven years now. When ego comes, love holes up.'

She was uncannily covered in an all white dress, only her face visible. Maru had never seen a nun, but it reminded him of the nurses he saw in the hospital.

Maru felt he was back in school. He went blank. He decided not to open his mouth. His nerves tensed and a sudden wave of pain passed through his spine.

She began after a brief pause, 'Like any other woman I also yearn to become a mother. But for my love I decided to sacrifice my motherhood. For a woman life means a lot. Having another being in her womb for nine months and then taking it out through a small crevice between her legs is what a woman is born for. To man, it is as simple as depositing his semen and putting claim over a readymade life.'

Maru felt he was dissolving in that darkness and turning into a ghost. He was no more a figure of flesh and blood. There was no pain in his neck. He felt he was invisible. He couldn't see more of her and the surroundings in that darkness.

'I know you have seeds in you. I am not sure if I am fertile or not. But I have found out if I am, then today is the most opportune day for me to get pregnant. You have to deposit some semen of yours into my womb for complete forfeiture.'

Maru knew that she wanted him to fuck her. He had lent his semen to many women till now without thinking even once that by doing that he could be having his offspring in this world; some more creatures like him.

She put gloves on her forehands and veiled her face. Her hands came out to hold and take Maru in her lap; he was standing still like a scared child. She pulled him closer to the bed and spread her legs to fit him in.

Maru was like a dead body straightened due to rigor mortis; no sign of life. She moved her hands all over his body. It was cold, no movement at all.

'You won't be able to do like this. Let me put the lights on.' She grinned.

She got up and switched on the bulb arching over a life size mirror. He could now partly see the interior of this big bed room. Darkness still reigned over the ambience. There were frames on walls and silhouetted figurines around in the room. He scanned the room till his gaze reached the mirror. He was transfixed. It was a reflection of a nude of hers hanging opposite the mirror. She was voluptuous; plump but distinctly curvaceous. Maru was in an imaginary world with surroundings apt to his ghostly existence. It was surreal and he felt lighter. His mind roved her body in the mirror and finally stopped at the eyes. She had the same look, the look of invitation in her eyes. He was excited. She looked into his face and smiled like a winner.

Maru suddenly felt as if he had broken open the treasury of a banished king with a magical key he had. All the wealth in it was now his. He was in a mood to plunder. First time in his life, he was ecstatic. He felt like screaming and splashing in the wave-pool. He felt like kissing and caressing her. He wished to go all over her smooth and supple body. He had so far experienced only those work-strained, bony women.

As he moved to hold her into his arms, she said, 'wait' and took the position on her bed. She could see his penis was ready to ignite the fire of life.

'You don't move. I will help you out.'

With her gloves on, she uncovered and took out his instrument with the precision of a confident operator. She fitted it into her vagina through a hole in her slacks she was wearing under her white gown. As Maru came forward to hold her waist, he was decently stopped.

'Begin now, Maru. But don't touch me at all. If you did that I will feel bad and stop it immediately.'

Maru was perplexed for a while. But had reached a stage from where a man can only go forward.

While he was at his work, she was giving words to her thoughts, 'Picture is an imagination. The nude woman in the painting is not me. It is my imagination. Sexuality is a perception. To you, I am sexy. To me, you are like any other man, only more simple and honest. Life is creation and that is real.'

Her words pricked his brain. For the first time he felt he should not have run away from school. How wonderful it would be to have knowledge of things, to know people, to know oneself and to express oneself to others. He felt he was divided into two. His lower half was moving back and forth; trying to go deep into her. His upper half was trying hard to listen to her, to understand her. He didn't know out of the two which one was he and which a ghost of him.

He closed his eyes to resist the temptation to touch her, gearing up his middle part into a rhythmic motion; in and out. It went fierce after a while.

First time he had an unstoppable urge to scream while ejaculating. But he tightened his jaw and finished without any sound.

'Hold it like this for a while.' The instruction came and he followed.

After two minutes, maintaining her posture, she said, 'You can go now. Complete your work if you want. Or you can do it whenever you feel like.'

She didn't move. Maru gathered himself, put his pyjamas in order and came out.

As he came into the real world, he realized that the ghost was back on its seat. He felt the stiffness in his neck and the pain was suddenly acute.

He came next day to complete the pending work. The landlord was also back.

Maru always remembered that day. It was the last time he had sex. His problem went on a quick escalation. In six months, the symptoms were visible to make known that it was not merely a neck problem. His facial feature showed signs of deformation. He realized that fate had a tougher task in store for him.

He found it difficult to continue working the way he did. Except for the long walk through the village to keep his limbs in motion he spent most of his time in his court yard. He would look at the sapling he planted after his mother's death, taking the shape of a tree.

His neighbour would come and keep some food for him. He knew that it was sent by landlord's wife. The landlord told him one day, 'Maru, it would be difficult for you to plough your two acres of land. I would suggest that you let me manage that and you will get your share of crop every season.'

Maru didn't say anything and the landlord without any paperwork took possession of the land. Life was pushing him more into ghostly reclusion.

While he was struggling to align with the reality, his neighbour told him one day that *madam* wanted to water the *peepal* tree in his courtyard for a month. He knew it was information in advance, and not a request.

Next day the lady came accompanied by the maid. She was in traditional attire. Her face half-veiled, eyes covered. She had a full blown belly. She was pregnant. Looking at her, Maru went suddenly into his ghost avatar. He felt she was real and he was just a soul.

Her prayers got heard and she gave birth to a male child. The whole village was invited to sing and celebrate the 6th night of the child's arrival. It was the night for the goddess of knowledge and success to come and write the fate of the newborn. Mother keeps a note-book and a pen underneath the pillow of the child. Maru was not sure his mother did that for him or not.

There was a grand feast after a month. Again the whole village was invited except Maru. A big basket of sweets came for him.

He observed, at times, women would stop at a distance if saw him on the way. They would not bring infants close to him. He took it not so seriously till he heard in whispers that his shadow could inflict a pregnant woman or an infant with this eerie ailment. He felt obscured. He would look at his own shadow for hours to examine its nasty character.

Maru now found his shadow more in existence than his real self. To him, his shadow was not a reflection of him rather he was an outcome of his shadow.

By the time landlord's son was five, Maru was in complete grip of the ailment. Maru had heard many stories about the child's princely upbringing, but had never seen the boy. People often said that the boy had his mother's face and father's built; an ideal combination. Maru desired to have one glance of the boy but the thought of his jinxed shadow always stopped him.

For better education, the boy was sent to his maternal house in the capital city. Away from the uncouth and rustic surroundings of the village, he was in an English medium school, meant for the rich and the royal. Maru never got another chance to hear the voice of the lady. He never again saw those eyes. Slowly and clumsily but the life went on. His contact to the world was through a few idlers and gossipers who never stopped visiting his ghostly house.

The old widow, an old friend of his mother and woman of dubious spiritual leanings often visited him but mostly when he was alone. Her young son died many years ago after a neck pain of a few weeks. His death was a mystery for years. It is still for the folks but the mother has uncovered the truth beyond doubt, she believes. Along that link, she has in her own way reached the genesis of Maru's problem as well. In every session she explained a part of the shrouded past. Maru got a better idea, day after day, what shadows are, and how ghosts descend this world life after life.

'It is your uncle, Maru. The world may not know the truth. But I can't fail to spot the rascal. I am a mother. He snatched away my 18 year old from me. I can never forgive the demon. My husband died of grief and I was left to suffer this widowhood. You wouldn't know all this. I don't even speak out the name of that rogue. They say if the name is uttered repeatedly by mortals, the sufferer in hell may get his salvation early. He remains there forever I pray.'

The old woman sounded sure of every word she spoke. At the same time conveniently swallowed a part, Maru often felt. Maru had known some of the facts she mentioned but he found her narration all the while puzzling. He would give her a stare to convey that he was not ready to take this hocus-pocus. She must clarify her claim. He would gape into her impregnable eyes to fish out the hidden text.

The woman would get her cue, 'you are alive today just because of your mother. She has been fighting like a tigress fights for her cub. Your uncle ran away from home at the age of thirteen. Your father searched him everywhere. There was no trace of him for eight years and was ultimately taken dead. The scoundrel came back. His occult past also came with him. He earned disrepute of a master of evil spirits. I only know how much he troubled your mother. She was a close friend, in fact, only friend I had. She tolerated him a hell. But after your father's death he crossed all his limits. He wanted to marry her. You were six months old. My son was three years older to you.'

Maru was all ears. The old woman was sorting out pieces of her secretly treasured tale. 'To take me on his side, the bastard would come and sweat talk with me.

Believe, my son, before striking the fate shuts the door from both the sides. I was trapped. Your mother warned me a few times. I apologize to her every day. But it is too late. All is lost.'

'There is something not to be told and not to be heard, my son. Your mother and I were hiding a sea in our chest. It was this scoundrel who pushed your mother from the roof. She didn't let him reach you. He took the revenge. Your mother had pushed him in the well. He is a soulless ghost. His soul is struggling in hell. Your mother's soul is still on this earth. She is around to protect you from his soulless ghost. She will not have her salvation till you are on this earth.'

Maru heard parts of her story in intervals, for months. He got many of the things about his past clear and had many more still unclear. He was not bothered whether he lives or dies. Time went on. He stopped stepping out of his house in day time. He would now take his long walk during the night.

It was the night before he decided to take a lifelong walk to the east. A walk to go away from the earth. Landlord's wife came to his house accompanied by her maid. Maru recognized her in a glance. After eighteen years she looked not much different.

It was almost midnight.

'So late', Maru mumbled.

'Yes, I had to.'

She signalled the maid to go while taking a seat on a corner of his cot.

My son is coming tomorrow for his vacation. He will now on spend time in the village to look after the land and the business. I want you to keep him defended from the evil spirits. You can only do that. I have sacrificed a lot to be a mother, you know.

She got up, bowed to him in respect and went out.

No one knows where Maru went. People believe he still walks around the village in the dead of night. He defends the village from evil spirits. Nobody has encountered any ghost since his disappearance. Time will only tell if a ghost comes back again to sit on a young neck. So far it's not.

The landlord now uses Maru's house for his animals. The lady started, and now everyone worships the *peepal* tree in Maru's courtyard.

LOVE STORY 1973-99

1973 was the year Chimanlal entered his degree course.

His mother's trite face was beaming with pride, 'A woman is her womb; her body is a facade. Beauty of a woman is seen in her progeny. In her sons. My Chiman has made me proud. I have no reason to curse my fate now.'

The women who heard her say this took in the emotion, but with a pinch of envy.

Leaving his village forty-nine kilometres behind—not approximately, but exactly going by the milestones of PWD, full form, Public Works Department—Chiman was bound to the district town of Rewari. He would now stay in the hostel of KPSPC, full form, Kasturmal Puranchand Somani Public College. India was in the grip of 'UNO' syndrome and not knowing full form of an abbreviation was an indefensible sign of poor GK. For the chic youngsters, the college was just *KPS*.

What Chiman did was a quantum leap, by any yardstick. No gainsaying, he added one more first to his name. In 100 plus *dasbhainsiya* clan of village Nangal Kheri, no one had till date climbed up the ladder of education to this height. And there was more to it. He did it with distinction—always stood first, hurdles of History and Geometry notwithstanding.

His mother's prophesy, she made at the end of every *macabre show,* was coming true, 'My Chiman will one day win for me to make good of my loss.'

His matriculation certificate read his name Chimanlal Dasbhainsiya. When had to tell (he preferred to avoid) he would keep it to Chimanlal. The surname '*dasbhainsiya*' never failed to amuse the audience and rarely got passed without a comment. He was happy that barring a few nasty guys in *KPS*, everyone called him Chiman. Chiman was a quaint name in this new world. Still it was any day less ridiculous than *dasbhainsiya.* Leg-pullers were out to scandalize it by putting extra stress on *dasbhainsiya.* What he wished—a kick on their ass. What he did—turned a deaf ear.

His family was always proud of owning more buffalos than anyone in the village. The legend holds that his great grandfather, at one time, became a distinguished owner of ten buffalos. People conferred on him the title of *dasbhainsiya* and the family fondly lapped up the honour. It eventually came to be their surname. Who would imagine that one day a boy from the generations to come would go to college to face embarrassment for a faux pas of his fore-fathers!

Just forty-nine kilometres away, but this was a different world. It had shops, buses, trains, cycle-rickshaws, motorcycles, not many but also cars, and a couple of cinema houses. No, this was a bloody formation for a cultural attack. The enemy was ubiquitously parading in bell-bottoms, printed shirts and long hair. It looked as if genders were about to cross lines.

Wise counsel announced, 'Culture is at stake.'

The generation in question had no time to heed.

In short, the new world had everything to transform a boy of eighteen into anything imaginable, and probably, into something unimaginable.

Chiman was missing what he left behind—the village and everything of the village. Its lanes, its folks, and the surroundings. And the temple! *You can't easily forget the cosiest place you played cards so very often.* He would now wait for a week or sometimes two to be nestled with the flock back home. Deracination can be devastating if not managed well. It has its charm, nevertheless. Partitions and exoduses have given birth to enigmatic tales and immortal love stories, inconceivable in normal times. Chiman had the pang of leaving his world behind, and at the same time, had the excitement of entering into an unfamiliar one. Cohabitation of two immiscible feelings in a pristine heart can put the life on a cliff-hanger. It did here as well.

Nothing seemed to be in place for some time. He was like a lost soul. After bewilderment and struggle of a few months he suddenly felt, 'I am in love!'

He looked around, searched his heart and scanned his surroundings, until he was sure—*it's nothing but love.*

The moment came he found himself in the grip of this strange feeling. It was so real that it would travel with him like a ring of light around his existence. It wouldn't let him connect to the greyish world outside of the halo. It was around him in the class room when he found the lecture dull and monotonous. It was there in the night, in that loneliness of the hostel when he would toss in his bed restlessly. At times it was so unbearable that he had to go and masturbate in the common bath room, to escape from this blessed confinement, and to hide into sleep. He was always aware of the guilt that would follow yet ready to take on the feeling of disgust that quickly follows the ejaculation.

'What the heck? In my thoughts, in my dreams—it's love, continuous love and nothing else than love. It's tearing me apart.'

And see the travesty; love's all around his existence yet it was not happening. Not having the object of longing in sight made the situation all the more critical. There had to be a girl—a special girl. The bugger went again for a first. Fell in love before finding the girl. Weird may it sound but true it was.

It was not as simple as made out here. *Yes, this is the age for a boy to fall into the honey-trap of this stinging life. The new world of magazines and cinema was taking its toll.* All this makes a good explanation in a normal case. It must be happening with most of the boys at that age. But they move ahead to grow out in life. For them, life goes into quandary for a while but it doesn't come to a screeching halt. For Chiman it did. It was a chasm deep within. He had no way to cope with it. Or the tribulation was perhaps the way also. It needs some deep digging to fathom the truth.

The boy grew up, hearing almost every day—'Chiman will earn a name.'

Some had taken a promise that he won't forget them once he was big and famous. Look, how sure they were. That was one part, the smaller one. On the other hand, the same boy helplessly watched his mother getting brutally beaten up by his father, every now and then. And trust, his father was not a wayward junkie. But when life decides to be bad there is nothing you can do to prevent its ghastly designs. That is the only answer you get if you think deeper. So there was a *macabre show*, every second day. He wouldn't know what to do, where to hide from this cruelty of life, in this uselessly vast universe.

But once you are grown beyond the child in you—you can't easily forgo, forget, or forgive. Everything keeps lingering. Everything comes back to haunt you. You are out of the fuel of *living innocently* nature fills up before pushing you out of the warm ensconces of a womb. You feel that you can't take things anymore. Your folks and your parents obliviously take you as the same innocent boy; you are now not. You want to rise up to the challenge. You have been nurturing a thought for quite some time, *'Once I am grown up I will set the life right for my parents and my siblings and for everyone who has a hope in me.'*

And you now believe is the time to turn that wish into reality. You begin to think, 'I will bring the prosperity and happiness and everything else that is needed to make mine a nice happy family. And also I will reach the heights people thought I would.'

You take a long flight to nowhere. And you find yourself alone standing across the abyss. You have no one with you. And it dawns upon you that you won't be able to do it alone.

'I need a companion.' You assertively tell yourself. You feel an urge to be complete.

I shall include her also henceforth.

Two of you together, in your distant imagination, make the best version of your hopeless parents. You can see the future like reality running right in front of you. You tell yourself again and again, 'I am in love with her. Men, women, birds, trees, stars, moon and you the sun, listen! I am in love with her!'

If you are in, you can well understand what Chiman was passing through.

'But where is 'she', my friend?'

The search began while Chiman was already in love.

Hope I have rightly put up Chiman's case, without making a war and peace of it.

Chiman's perception of beauty was no different from anyone with a rustic upbringing. There was a regular march of live beauty in those lanes overrun by buffalos, cows and camels. Girls are one concept of beauty there—wheatish, chiselled and dove-eyed, with a good framework to hold a curvaceous body in offing. And then there are women—healthy, wholesome, toned-up, and free, with an inviting gait. Chiman had seen enough of both. He had in his imagination a girl, with some acceptable combinations and variations that could make that 'she'. The challenge was to find her in *KPS*.

It was a disappointing search to begin with. Admissions were still on in some faculties; there was a hope. Would you believe that there was not a single one who gave, once at least, that fucking 'eureka' feeling no matter if later fails on a stricter scrutiny? There was not even one girl close to his imagination. Sad! The slot was created. Love had happened. A right girl was must, and the scope was limited.

Chiman did a second round, this time with a closer but lenient eye. He registered a few faces and put them aside in his mind to make the final choice easier. Like women do while selecting the best dress from many on the racks. The choice looks always limited.

It was no fun. If a girl had beautiful eyes her body was very frail.

'I don't know why these young girls always eat like they are unwelcome guests in this world. They never have a desire to grab things like the boys do. Some have a figure that stuns you but in best case too body can't make up for face; certainly not in case of a girl; a would-be bride.'

He would attentively—posing casually—stand at the main gate at apt timings. Beginning with an eye contact is the time-tested way. He used it, instinctively. He did his best to create a chance for the eyes to meet, if couldn't, evaluated with whatever came in the view. He saw all of them a few times, and a few of them many a times.

'There's only one my mind keeps going back to, time and again.'

She was not the 'it' thing, but had something in her that grows upon slowly like an unfamiliar fragrance.

You have to just feel it every time with a higher degree of concentration. After a few attempts, you get it. But once you have got it; you have got it. Let the whole world say it's not so great but that will not change your mind. Your view against the view of the rest makes you more convinced of your special sense, others, you feel, utterly lack.

He gazed every feature of her, for a few days until he was sorry, 'Oh God! How come I have missed such a fine work of the nature in my first assessment? Shame upon me!'

Love was at work.

The subtlety of her indefinable beauty gave him a scope to forgive himself for his rustic perception. In a week's time he felt she was, truly speaking, a tad above his imagination. She was perfect, his imagination was not.

Fair, slim, and tall. That is just the basic. She was much more. The nature's way of defining elegance! And her simplicity?

So simple that, '*I can easily see her soul through her eyes. What she lacks is distinct curves and a bit of plumpness. But that will come with the time. And the time has begun to come. I will see more of her and I will know more of her. I, the true lover, deserved this divine favour I am sure. Good things don't happen so quickly, so easily.*'

She had a modest appearance and that spoke of her good parentage.

'*What should be her caste? Can be a gujjar like me?*' Wait!

'*Screw it. Love knows no caste. I will set an example. It shouldn't cross the swords of religion. As far as you have common gods, you can always cope. Let me get ready for the next move.*'

Life looked better. Classes were not so dull. No masturbations since there was no trepidation needing this self-help tranquilizer.

He now missed his village and his folks lesser and lesser. He found a better thing to do on weekends than elbowing for space in a packed state transport bus, followed by a brisk walk of 2.5 kilometres, to join the horde back home. Looking for her in the crowded market, in temples, and wherever a college girl could possibly hang around on a weekend, was an exciting option. He also needed to be away from those sudden bursts of the '*macabre show*'. The life he was planning on a green plot of imagination had no place for such disgrace.

To alleviate himself, he had the alternative of welling up his eyes for his helpless mother, sitting in a corner, 49 kilometres away, if guilt caught up. *For god's sake, he was not loafing around here. He was trying his best to sort out the mess of a life he inherited.* It was not easy to hate a father who was so nice at times.

'There's no end to my predicament. My love is not a luxury.' He would convince himself.

'*The fair, slim, and tall will one day take charge of my life. That will be the beginning of my dreams turning into reality. I know I'm intelligent; my school record is a testimony. I have will power. I can do anything to prove myself once the stage is set. It's not so difficult to become a Nobel laureate, an Olympian, or a film-star or a prime minister. Let the right person, now in sight, take command of my life. Everything will fall in place.*'

Hail love!

It was now time to know more about the *fair, slim, and tall* before taking the journey through her eyes to her soul. She was also from science stream. It took a good one week to just know her name.

Here came a bolt from the blue. Harsh truth is something we don't believe for a while even if there's no reason to doubt. Like it happens when a news of death comes all of a sudden. One wishes the news to be untrue. It's mostly not. Her name was Gurmeet Kaur.

Gurmeet Kaur! The road took a sudden turn into an unknown territory. Gurmeet Kaur, his soul-mate! A Sikh girl to be the bride of *dasbhainsiya* clan. He was ill-equipped to continue with his dream. The sets, the properties, the costumes, the content, everything he had in his thoughts were absurdly misfit to deal with the incongruity he saw in 'Kaur'. Names, made out of a few meaningless characters, have the potential to screw up the happiness of your life. How bizarre! His visualization would go blank the moment he tried to move ahead with his thoughts. His mind was like a photo reel exposed before putting into the camera. It appeared unreal, impossible!

Such are His ways. Fate had another big first for him in store, the warning was clear. With a long sigh he exhorted himself to rise up to the challenge. Her image was like a permanent fixture, painted on the inner walls of his mind while the name Gurmeet Kaur incessantly whacked his head. He agonisingly wished if her name could be changed into one that sounds a melody to his ears. Not necessarily a name of his choice. Anything that sounded regular was good enough. A mere name stood like a mountain in the way of true love, what a pity. *No way Chiman*!

An undesirable name for a beautiful flower! It is bound to sound harmonious if you appreciate the flower in every breath and your heart keeps breaking the name in syllables, and constantly murmurs it. It took a few days to set the problem right. He took a sigh of relief as it reached—*Meet!* It was making perfect sense; *Meet*—the soul-mate. Oh God! I can't believe you could be so quizzical. Sucked into quick sand, about to drown, and he came back to the shore with a strong returning wave. *Saved!*

The fear of ominous call was lingering. He helped his head to ignore it. Or was he moving ahead with it? There was no going back. He saw his fate coming. It was like a whirlwind. What was in the envelope of dust, he had no clue. Closer to him was a face always turning into a flower, the moment he closed his eyes.

It was now the time to fly around the flower. Passionately. Sipping the nectar is ultimate in true love. The campus of *KPS* was the Garden of Eden to him. Just he and she, and none else. The crowd would suddenly turn into images to mingle up with trees and shrubs, silently swinging with the wind. His day would start with a blissful sight of her face. Invigorated, he would joyously attend his class.

Missing a glimpse of her was a sad and bad start of a day.

The circumference of his revolution around her was shrinking with every new day. The *radius of the circle of love* got fixed once she noticed him and gave a return look. He won't shorten it further he knew. This was partly for the respect he had for her tightly held persona and partly for the dignity of his love. But he went out of the way to see her a few times in day, only for his innocently obstinate heart. Mostly at the cost of a couple of lectures he had to miss.

'You can make up for the lessons you missed but a moment lost in love is irredeemable.'

She would look back at him, nonchalantly, once a while. It was difficult to make out her feelings, her response.

It was certainly not a 'no' and that was enough for a true lover to stake his future; his life.

It was a sunny day of winter season that would arrive in a few years from now. Two of them were sitting together on a secluded bench in a lawn looking similar to that of KPS. They chatted about anything and everything of life. Except the 'macabre show'. He had buried it in a dark corner of his mind to hide it forever from Meet. They were happy that they could 'together' gracefully deal with the religion issue. That was really a wonderful feat. It had set an example for the people living . . . no, barely surviving in a repressive world.

These mountainous problems have cool answers when two lovers sit and talk, aloof from this world.

Parents from both sides caved in, after some resistance, of course (his with more but had to). Dressed like a bride (it's a Hindu wedding), she came into his life.

A flash of when they would be employed as professors in the same college.

Both have to get ready for the college at the same time. Chiman was told off every day for his lazy ways and lousy manners. Particularly for not wiping off the bath room properly. It wouldn't even if he tried his best. The bickering will go on sometimes. Love played a great referee at the end.

Cut to . . . *He treats her like a fairy queen . . . They had two kids . . . in jump cuts. He wished sons both. Chauvinism deep in his blood won't allow him to agree for a girl. But for the love of his 'Meet' he settled for one daughter. A nice and complete family. The 'macabre show' disappeared as horns went from donkey's head. She became the queen-bee of dasbhainsiya clan. Life was like it couldn't have been better.*

While all this was happening . . . please note. While all this was happening, he never ever undressed her in his imagination even for once. He had in fact never seen her beyond her anklets. Can you believe it? And they had two kids. This happens only in true love. A true lover never imagines unbuttoning his beloved; not even after he has really done it.

In real life, that moment was still far for Chiman. Very far perhaps.

Love was there for real. What more a proof, the world would need? Chiman—on records Chiman Lal Dasbhainsiya—was a true lover. The truth needs to be saved before it finds its way to the graveyard of history.

Let's not forget Chiman had a poor sense of History. He could never put the events in right chronological order. He fell in love before meeting the girl. Not only that, he went ahead to visualise his marriage with her, and had two lovely kids. Walking on the earth, he was yet to exchange a word with her. He had no idea of the cruel games of fate. Those who try to run ahead of time are mercilessly overrun. Chiman had in his dream-run jumped the gun of time. We may wish him good luck, at this critical junction.

Constantly revolving in his orbit, he felt like a sole moon of the sole earth. Nothing else existed in his universe. No sun, no planets and no stars. There was vacuum around, he did feel at times. But he had no clue of the black holes; more powerful than the visible mass and energy. He had no imagination of the inter-galactic void that separates one cluster of stars from the other. He did feel the pang of separation, though. There was love, and there was a distance, he knew.

The distance was maintained with reverence.

The next hurdle.

He had pathetically poor grasp of Geometry of human relations that was out there to suck him in. He was unaware. From any point of the circumference you may look to the centre, it is constant attraction. It's love. But for the one who looks from centre to the circumference and finds the same person again and again at various points, it's objectionable. It's stalking, to be more precise. Walking along the piously drawn circumference, Chaman could never figure out a difference between love and stalking.

Not even after the fateful day she suddenly stopped and spoke to him for the first time.

Her carriage was of a child admonishing an elder. 'You seem to be from a good family. Why don't you put your mind into studies?' She finished and walked away without waiting for his reaction.

She had rehearsed her lines a few times, it appeared. Chiman had no words. He was not prepared. Her words were chiming in his abruptly blanked mind till much after she was gone.

She had still not said 'no', he realized all of a sudden. Yes . . . it was not a no. It was more of a conditional 'yes' in his interpretation. He rephrased her words, 'if you are from a good family . . . *I believe you are* . . . and over that if you concentrate on your studies and do well . . . *I will consider you.*' He rounded it off with just two ifs.

'*Is it not an oblique way, a discreet way, a girl's way, to say, 'I like you'?*' It is, of course. He agreed with his heart.

He obeyed her. Came out of his orbit, and went into his books often. He could not keep himself away. Sometimes through clouds and sometimes from somewhere below the horizon, he was back into the orbit. He would go out and come back, incessantly.

How atrocious will it be for a young man in love to study the names and structures of human bones—radio-ulna, tibio-fibula . . . completely inane!

Doctor! Chiman, a doctor?

His family's dream was merely a reflection of dreary ambitions, he sighed.

'I can't see myself a doctor, not at all after this elegiac interlude. 'Meet' is the best person to decide. Let me park this career thing aside for the time being.'

'There is a poet in me, a restless poet, someone knows?'

Perhaps no one! Certainly no one!

There can't be anything more torturous for parents to see their son a budding poet. All poetic ambitions have to be, therefore, nourished surreptitiously, like love. Love and poetry live close to each other, no wonder.

Hindi poetry is too commonplace to express an exceptional love. Chaman was sure his was. It has to be something no commoner understands. Something deeply meaningful; lying in some dark chamber of literature, to be unearthed for this solemn occasion. Something like he had read but never really understood. He imagined himself in the league of those great poets of love. He had a feeling—desperately in want of words—to be expressed; words that can wrench out truth of a heart in love. It is something so universal that everyone has his own connection with; alike and still unique from everyone else's.

Library was the next logical destination.

Seniors and professors were amused to see a junior from science stream digging into English literature section. Such a deep plunge of a student from *KPS* into this 'out of syllabus' English poetry was prima facie an act of conceit. It made everyone look around at least once to figure out if it was a charade. *Is it a gambit to eye up a girl?* God forgive those mortals having no clue that Chiman was not available for such nonsense. He was now beyond all this. There was no scope left for such frivolity his life. He flipped through the books he guessed had the verses to match the feelings in his heart.

After a long search he got it. It was a love poem of John Donne—a love song in fact. He read it a few times. Though not very clear, but sounded reflective of his state of mind. Some parts were reading not so relevant. The depth, flow and rhyme brought it still closer to his state of mind. That is the magic of poetry. He took out a note-book to copy it down.

Sweetest love, I do not go,
For weariness of thee,
Nor in hope the world can show
A fitter love for me;
But since that I
Must die at last, 'tis best
To use myself in jest
Thus by feign'd deaths to die.

Yesternight the sun went hence,
And yet is here today;
He hath no desire nor sense,
Nor half so short a way:
Then fear not me,
But believe that I shall make

Speedier journeys, since I take
More wings and spurs than he.
O how feeble is man's power,
That if good fortune fall,
Cannot add another hour,
Nor a lost hour recall!
But come bad chance,
And we join to'it our strength,
And we teach it art and length,
Itself o'er us to'advance.

When thou sigh'st, thou sigh'st not wind,
But sigh'st my soul away;
When thou weep'st, unkindly kind,
My life's blood doth decay.
It cannot be
That thou lov'st me, as thou say'st,
If in thine my life thou waste,
That art the best of me.

Let not thy divining heart
Forethink me any ill;
Destiny may take thy part,
And may thy fears fulfil;
But think that we
Are but turn'd aside to sleep;
They who one another keep
Alive, ne'er parted be.

Let the death come and go
I will be thine forever
And when the world will turn
The pages of the history of mankind

You will be there with me
There with me, you will be.

He tore the leaf out and kept in his pocket to read it, and read it, and read it. He wouldn't know that this love song of John Donne that sounded so aligned to his mood had his fate written in it. True that a poet reaches where light has not yet. And the future is where light has not reached yet. Unknown and unwritten. Chiman got a glance of his future. It looked bright. There's darkness deep down into the bright universe. No one can see it from here.

He read it nearly hundred times in next one week. It was now his poem and not John Donne's. More he read more he felt this song was fated to convey his love. It was very long he felt. But he couldn't find a word he should have deleted.

'*Passing a slip to a girl was an indecent overture. But if you understand good things, pure and divine—every word and its meaning here was—then you have to agree that a moron would only call it indecent. In fact, a beloved shall be obliged to read such a profound and honest expression of a lover.*' He exalted himself.

'She must read it'—was the cry from the heart bellowing in his chest until he agreed to slip the paper into the crevice of the bench, Meet and her friend regularly occupied in the class. He folded it many times to fit the cleft, and with trembling fingers accomplished the solemn act. It will go as a mute communication in the history, so sure he was of the depth of the poem that came out from John Donne and journeyed to be once again penned by Chiman.

To his dismay, it was a scandal the next day. People need scandals like plants need carbon-dioxide for their survival. If they don't have it around, they have a method to create it. *Meet* took out the slip right under the nose of her benchmate. They saw it a dirty mischief of one of the many eve-teasers in the class. These cheap nuts needed a good lesson. The benchmate was impatiently looking for a chance. She was sick of the unsavoury comments, she mostly overheard about herself.

She had no mind to guess if the lines written on this folded paper had some deep meaning; asking to be fathomed out. As she read the first two words—*sweetest love*, she screamed 'cheap nonsense' and snatched the crumpled paper away from *Meet*.

In no time, it was in the hands of Professor Rustogi, an authority on mathematics and equally so on discipline. If he had a say the word discipline would be in the preamble of our constitution, in bold capitals. The news travelled at the speed of conjunctivitis. It was everywhere. Chiman got to hear it from all who had a tongue.

'What did he want, a fuck? Right! Then what's the need to be so twisty for a straight thing.'

'Yes, you're right. The poor girl gave it to Professor Rustogi because she couldn't understand it. And the problem is no one still understands it. So the lesson is—be simple and straight like a dick and not deep and difficult like a cunt.'

'I think they should let him go for his great piece of poetry.'

'No, boss, no! This I don't agree. We should know at least who this John Donne is in our KPS.'

Chiman knew he was in a terrible mess. His only support was his love.

In next couple of days he felt that he was everyone's topic. They knew him or they knew him not. It was like people were trying to identify a lone star, by nothing else than its lonely location in the sky. The principal laughed his heart out when Professor Rustogi suggested that the culprit should be traced and rusticated from the college.

'Culprit! I think it's a right word professor, poetically speaking. You must trace him out. In fact I would like to have a chat with him. But why rusticate him? Let a poet bloom in this culturally barren environment of KPS. No?'

Professor was more annoyed than disappointed.

The crumpled piece of paper was passed on to the henchmen, always ready for a purge under the one-line instruction of Professor Rustogi. Chiman had no clue.

The matter eventually landed into the hands of a foursome. Balvinder Singh, a cousin of Gurmeet Kaur, a *five-k sikh* and a weightlifter of the college, was one of them. The second was his friend, a drop out who still dropped in, now and then to give company to his friends. The third was this friend's friend, no one knew who he was, and why he was coming to the college so often when not enrolled here. And the last one was nobody's friend, a failed boxer always ready to use his failed skill on people's face. Chiman's face was shown to them by a class-fellow who after checking the handwriting concluded that the poetic lecher was none other than the 'aloof star'. *Meet*, her *whistleblower* friend and professor Rustogi were left alone where they were.

It was now Chiman's turn to be stalked. It took place before not many days passed, at an early hour of a night when he was on his way to the hostel.

They told him, 'Come aside of the road, *Romeo*. We would like to have an urgent word with you.'

Chiman could guess what the word was about. For him, all the words put together were not equal to the one word—love.

Balvinder took out the crumpled paper from his pocket.

'Who has written this?'

The poem tidily written by him on a pristine piece of paper was by now a sullied rag violated by many uncouth hands. For a while Chiman was in agony for the passage he chose. Lowly way for a heavenly purpose. *Mistaken*.

He gave it a sombre look before saying, 'I have written this.'

'Do you know the meaning of this?' At every question they gazed into one another's eye, to match their expressions. And while doing this, the four of them together looked like one octopus like animal with eight eyes.

'Yes, of course', he was firm and polite. It made the eight-eyed beast furious.

It pounced on Chiman with its eight arms; the boxer's two lobbed non-stop and the remaining six came turn by turn. Every thrash came with a word of abuse. Chiman kept quiet till fallen unconscious. The *octopus* went away.

It took him hours to regain consciousness. The boxer had smashed his head hard. Chiman was feeling giddy. His face had lumps all over, he touched and felt. It should be blue with clots of blood, he could guess. Yes, it was more than he imagined. It was not a beating that could be hidden. He was clear.

He went to the hostel in a state of trance. Hostellers went out to complete their story without enquiring what really happened.

News reached Nangal Kheri against Chiman's wish. His attempt to keep himself confined in his room couldn't stop the spread.

'Chaman had a fatal attack on him. He is saved simply because the luck was on his side. The danger is still hovering around him.' The deduction was not baseless. Rest of the details came as wild guesses; and no wonder the story changed from one thing to another in every narration.

'Fifty! It should be close to fifty if you count all the able bodied males in dasbhainsiya clan.' In no time all of them were ready with their harvesting tools; now weapons. They were ready to turn KPS a battlefield. Victim will be whosoever came in their way.

Chiman's granduncle, a man known for his worldly wisdom, announced in his sonorous voice, 'No! Calm down. I have heard it's a matter of a girl. Anybody's girl's everybody's daughter. Our Chiman is a gem of a boy, no doubt. But any thoughtless move will ruin the girl's life.'

Mention of girl brought the tempers down. Enraged faces were suddenly pensive.

'We will settle score with the ma'fucker rogues later. We should safely bring Chaman home first.' Another sober pronouncement came to lead the opinion.

'Yes, before the dawn, Chiman should be here.' Consensus came with a voice vote.

Chiman was whisked away from the hostel in an ambush operation, in the dead of that very night. The only witness, his room-mate, was found gagged and tied-down to his bed, next morning.

It was a kidnap everyone believed. This must be a chain action by the same set of ruffians who thrashed up Chiman, many ranted. No one went to the police. All waited for Chiman's family to come and report the matter. That was never to be.

Rumour-mongers had a free run. Murder came a strong possibility by one of the many theories floating around.

The foursome ran like rats do, from one hole to another, in face of a flood. The crumpled paper Balwinder still had in his possession was an incriminating document; an evidence of the murder they never committed.

The paper went back to Professor Rustogi as an unspoken plea to now stand up as a saviour of his gullible followers. He dithered, yet under obligation, took charge of the piece of poetry. He had no choice than to pass it back to the brash friend of Gurmeet, with a sad yet supportive statement, 'The principal is scared of taking a moral stand. But you can take my word if the culprit is caught I will never let him continue in this college.'

And to complete its reverse journey, the paper came back to its originally intended recipient. For some reason, Gurmeet, *the Meet,* went to, but stopped, before tearing it into pieces; though destroying was a better option than preserving, under the given circumstance. Shredding it gave her a feeling that the writer was no more. She wished he is alive.

Someone's expression of love to you is your most personal and cherished gift in life. Meet came to realize as she thought again and again about the poem she had not read complete. And she was now sure of it, holding the crumpled paper in her hand. She softly moved her fingers on it, to smoothen it, to accept it. When someone loves you so purely and sincerely; who's that someone is immaterial. You have the feeling of heavenly bask. Your conscience may allow you to ignore the call of reciprocation. Nevertheless you feel like you are a special child of the destiny. Moving ahead in life with such feeling is a privilege. It was Gurmeet's that day.

She wouldn't go for the love she was tendered but she wouldn't discard it. She will keep it as a gift she never asked for; she never expected, yet got. After neatly folding the paper she kept it at a place she believed was easy to forget. She wished to remember the feeling forever and she wished to forget the incident forever.

Chiman was kept in internment till he completely recuperated. Some blue marks persisting on the sides of his face were a reminder to the avengers of *dasbhansiya* clan of their pending pledge. In spite of all his explanations and arguments Chiman was not allowed to go back to KPS. His family was unmoved. He lost his year.

Next year he was sent to a newly opened Government College in Ateli Mandi, merely 6 kilometres from Nangal Kheri. Chaman was given a new bicycle to daily commute the distance. The new college was short of faculty, short of building and short of everything. He was still a promising boy, worth everyone's emotional investment. He was still a blue-eyed boy of the clan, but had lost his chooser's status. The reality of life was catching up.

Not possible that Chiman wouldn't think about committing suicide at this point, burdened with a feeling of heavy loss. He did. After a few fake attempts he realized it was a borrowed feeling from a cheap love story; his love would never warrant.

His universe faced a big crunch before it came back into motion. After an excruciating pain of months, *Meet* went a few layers down into his mind. His pain and anger were slowly changing into inspiration and determination. He would do the impossible; something the world will always remember. His life was turning into an unstoppable force. His love for *Meet* was shaping into a perpetual engine running on inexhaustible fuel. He wouldn't get his *Meet*. He would now go farther in love. He could live with the *Meet* residing deep down in his soul and without one he saw for months from his orbit of attraction.

'*Macabre show*' stopped for a change. And stealthily came back one fine morning as if was hiding in a dark corner of the house. Life was on a miserably slow track.

Chiman was a jailbird. Future was limited; clearly visible from anywhere he saw.

He will conveniently get his graduation degree; he studies hard or not. That would seamlessly take him to a one-year degree course—the bachelor of education. And in a few years from now he will be a science teacher, like many graduates around. Any reasonably well-to-do and respectable father from Gujjar community will go out of his reach to fetch this dream son-in-law. The girl will be a gazelle-eyed, in all probabilities another *fair, slim and tall,* overwhelmingly respectful, and a matriculate; a perfect *bride* the clan could dream of. It was all set for a routine and decent life ever after.

Chiman will not say 'no' to any of this. Chiman will still achieve the highest a true love can ever do. He felt like a logwood in a river longing to meet a destiny different from the river's.

Oh gosh! It went more or less like he feared. He was a science teacher in a nearby village, Pali. He got married to a girl who was not expecting anything from life except a small thing—happiness. Happiness for her innocent heart and for everyone around. Her arrival was a wonderful thing; a fairy tale like. Chiman was grateful. He had no right to disappoint this *pari* descended from a land of all virtuous things. Not at all when he realized that after her auspicious entry, the *macabre show* went away to never come back, perhaps.

Life's traps were laid to make his heart a graveyard where a love was lying buried and a family garden was being created. A great achievement was the only way to break the shackles.

Life was good, but to her bafflement, Vimla found her husband mostly struggling. He would study late nights or run around to fill up some forms. She wouldn't understand why he should do all this when had a stable and respectable job. And over that, acres of land and everything one needs to lead a good life. She took care of Chiman like he was a king of their small kingdom and she a queen and a servant rolled into one. Chiman was embarrassed at times. In his thoughts he didn't deserve this reverence and pampering. His scarred love and her spotless devotion were a bit mismatch; all else being fine, in spite of.

Chiman was very soft and caring to her. She was like a goddess to him. There was guilt in him, he was always aware of. He never even spoke the word 'love' to another woman, leave aside a relationship but had been in love before getting married. No denying. It would fade away with time but only if he let it. With a haunting past behind, he loved his wife for all he was worth. He needed to drown to go to the other shore, he always felt. It was tiring at times but love never lets you feel tired.

He was a school teacher. Life was like a bird walks for some time in a day to cross very small distances from one grain to another. It has to otherwise keep flying to go where it wants to, or to go nowhere but just to be on its wings and reach high in the air. The reality began to descend on him that the time closes all the doors one by one as you grow older. It became clear one day when he heard from a teacher in his school that a *sikh* girl from Rewari got selected to Indian Administrative Services. His hunch was right. She was none other than his *Meet*. He was happy for her and sad for himself. Her words chimed in his ears.

Life had dumped him he felt. We would have to do something greater, much greater. The time to achieve in the worldly routine was gone. *I have no liberty to stake my life. I have a very innocent and pure woman whose fate is tied with mine.* He would read one thing, and think this, and read another. There was so much around to be happy and there was a speck deep within, heavy enough to make him sad at the end. *I will have to achieve without creating a ripple of disturbance.* He went further into books. Everyone wondered what he was studying now when his time to study was over. He would write poetry that made him feel light and aroused hope of becoming a poet the world would salute one day. He had studied basic physics and had a dream to fathom the ultimate truth of this universe. A light years long shot would look real to him. Or it would perhaps take him light years away from that heavy speck of gravity sucking him constantly in. He would read theory of relativity and quantum mechanics with a streak of pain. Had he read all this at right time, things would have been different. Her words chimed again.

He had many feats, any one ever had in the small world he dwelled. He had many firsts to his name. Every achievement of his looked great as it came, and after a while it looked like a pebble thrown in the pond. Some ripples, and over. It began with his first poem published in a local Hindi magazine after he sent hundreds to national level periodicals. Poetry makes one feel stripped in the public; benign praise it might bring. You simply make your heart bare to everyone. It's more so when the writing not really great, inexplicably great. A stage came he would write and keep hidden till the time it begins to sound impersonal.

He went to science with vengeance to remove the facade of illusion nature had around it. He wanted to bring God out of the unknown. No one has ever done on this earth. He wrote articles on, in fact against, every set principle of science. A few got published. He could see a possibility of a Nobel Prize. IAS is an apology in front of the Nobel. He would fly and come back to his nest every day. A place his wounded heart always got respite, and also energy to take on the next struggle. Vimla was first a companion in his fight, and then slowly turned into his inspiration to excel.

One day in a moment of weakness he felt so close to her and opened his heart.

'You think I am good-looking and desirable?'

'No! . . . you are more than that.' Vimla was jovial.

'Can you believe there was a girl in my college who just trashed me? Didn't find me worth having a word with?'

'She was not having luck greater than mine so she lost you to me. Simple.'

'She is an IAS officer now and I a mere teacher.'

Vimla noticed his pain. It was reflecting in his eyes.

'You can't achieve happiness. You have it or you don't have it. I have it by the grace of my teacher. I don't know about her.'

She was simple yet meaningful, he marvelled.

And she cautiously went to prod. 'Do you have it or you're missing it.'

'What?' he had lost the cue.

'Happiness'

'I am more than happy, my love! I am lucky too. But that's not enough. One has to achieve to make up for the loss one has in life. That's the human spirit.'

'It means you are not happy. But I will make you forget what you don't have. Name, fame or whatever you are missing.' She didn't want to utter the word, love. Her words to cheer him had motherly concern.

Time went and Vimla gave birth to a son. The family's joy had no bounds. Chiman's mother saw the pinnacle of happiness before dying of sudden chest pain. The stress she had for years took its toll. Every one said, 'How lucky Sarbati was. Saw all good things of life before departing.'

The boy was named Bheem. For no other reason but her grandmother wished so. In her belief, no single devil or a group of them would ever dare to hit my grandson like some beasts did to my son. She could never forget though the avowed avengers did with the passage of time. They rather made joke out of it to tease Chiman at times.

A time came Chiman was a highly regarded teacher in the region. A respected teacher might mean big in a small world but is very small in this big world.

Chiman kept, without any serious efforts, track of *Meet's* life though never had a compelling desire to go and see her. There was a great galactic space between them; only imaginable, not traversable.

Gurmeet was married to a Foreign Services officer of her batch, a *mona sikh* from Punjab. Both were settled in Delhi. She was with Home Ministry and Mr Kahlon was an attaché de mission with the Ministry of External Affairs. He was posted abroad for a long time; first as an attaché and then as a diplomat. Now in the list to become a full-fledged ambassador. Meet was a Joint Secretary, paved to be the Home Secretary of India one day. Chiman was a science teacher and the only thing that would happen in his career was quite foreseeable; he would be a Headmaster before his retirement. The story ends there.

Chiman would not let it be, so easily. He was 40 and his son was 8.

Time was getting over for him. If no break through comes; he would do a supreme sacrifice. He will give away his life for the nation. Nothing can be bigger than this. He would often ruminate; delusional it might be.

He would then think of Vimla, and of Bheem, and come out of his reverie. They will be shattered, left alone in a big world. They will be perhaps one day proud of his sacrifice. It was a harsh thought. He could do some act of exemplary courage and survive to see the day of glory. He would think every time he saw the home minister of the country making a helpless statement after every terrorist attack. Meet would be writing these hollow statements and preparing these verbose reports a common man is sick of hearing every day, he would imagine.

It reminded him of his failed attempt with Services Selection Board, to become a commissioned officer in the army. He soon chanced upon an advertisement to be an officer in the Territorial Army; an also-ran and a very peripheral wing of the country's defence. If he goes for it, people will laugh at his stupidity. It was meant for laggards even a villager knew. He clandestinely applied for a two years stint and decided to tell Vimla only after the call for the physical test and interview comes.

His half-hearted attempt got him selected, to his surprise. He had no choice than to reveal it now.

Eye-brows were raised. Some called it a silly step of a confused teacher. He convinced Vimla. 'It was my dream since childhood to be a soldier and it's just a matter of two years.'

She accepted his statement without accepting his reason.

The fate was still not favouring. As it came to the posting in action-packed region of Poonch border, he lost his bid for reasons unknown in spite of choosing to be the part of a small group of willing takers. Opportunity was still away. It may never come. Vimla had not ever stayed a week away from him. This was going to be a long separation. She cried a lot while giving Chiman a farewell; tears rolling down on a broad smile; heart-breaking yet auspicious. He must call her up every alternate day was the promise.

His unit was despatched to a desolate post in the border district of Ganganagar. It gave a feeling of banishment. Sand dunes were spread till the eyes could see. After the ritual of training every morning Chiman would teach basic science to jawans. Teritorial Army found a use of his qualification. His real wish was not there on the record. It was in his heart. He felt he has come farther from his already distant goal in life. He was regretting his decision. Life is not to chase mirages.

He didn't know the next that happened in *Meet's* life. Mr Kahlon was caught by CBI while passing on some classified information to wrong people and was arrested. Meet took it first as a jealousy trap against a promising officer. But as revelation came with every investigation report, she had to believe what she never would have liked to. Her husband was deep into it. He had fallen for his weakness for women. His handlers took advantage of it and dragged him more and more into the mire while he was lusting.

It brought raids not only to them but their near ones as well followed by ignominy she had not seen in her worst thoughts. Meet was broken. Kahlon faced all this with a brass neck. Meet realized for the first time in her life that she hardly knew the man she was married to and had a daughter from. She decided to bring herself out of the foul mess and keep her daughter away from the shadows of disgrace she would be inheriting. Separation.

She built her house in the town of Rewari where she was born and brought up. Every vacation she was there with her daughter. From Gurmeet Kahlon, she became Gurmeet Kaur once again.

Against all odds, Chiman struck big, truly big this time. He won it by miles this time leaving everyone in the game much behind. The news was all over the television; he was in the headlines. Chiman was dead. He was a household name overnight. Everyone wanted to know the detail. Hearts bled.

Blaring screams of pain and stoning silence of loss were in conflict all over the village Nangal Kheri. Chiman's father was sitting like a statue of ash. Like you touch and it will collapse. Vimla was woodened. Attempts to make her cry failed. Someone brought Bheem and asked him to hold her hand. It didn't work. An old woman unwittingly said, 'Chiman has not died he has become a martyr.'

A sole tear emerged in her eye and before it dropped a cry came from her heart. She inconsolably howled for long. Women reminisced Chiman's mother, 'Sarbati was really fortunate that she's not here to see this day of unbearable grief.'

A group of three terrorists wearing fatigues sneaked into the BSF camp. In a burst of firing 6 jawans were laid dead while the terrorists reached a vantage position on the second floor of the building. Officers and jawans ran wantonly till there was an abrupt silence. Intermittent sound of gunshots came from the corner terrorist were hiding.

Second Lieutenant Chiman was having his nap in a tent next to the barrack allocated to new recruits of Territorial Army. There was no rifle around and it would have been of little use against the automatic weapons the terrorists had. He had only a preliminary training in use of hand grenades. He gathered his courage and rushed to the ammunition room. Picked up six hand grenades and climbed up the tree. The window of the second floor room where the terrorist were closeted was around 10 feet from him. He activated all the grenades one by one and threw them in the room. There was a spray of bullets from the terrorists. After 10 minutes of heavy action, it was a pin drop silence. No one in the camp knew what really happened. They only realized when found the body of 2nd Lt Chimanlal underneath the tree. The three terrorist were found dead in the second floor room.

Chiman's cremation was the biggest event the region had ever witnessed. It was with the stately honour with a gathering of more than twenty thousand raging atmosphere with slogans—Shahid Chiman ! Amar Rahe! . . . Bharat Mata Ki Jai.

The news was picked up by all national channels. Newspapers covered it extensively. Almost everyone from dasbhainsiya clan saw his face on the TV. Some were interviewed by the news reporters. Bheem was around in most of the visuals. Vimla, in spite of heavy persuasion, didn't come in front of the camera.

Immense pride couldn't assuage the profound grief of a father. Chiman's father didn't survive to see Chiman's posthumous coronation with Ashok Chakra, the highest gallantry award of peace time. Vimla along with Bheem went to attend the investiture ceremony on the republic day.

Vimla was in trance when Chiman's name was announced and she walked up to the President of India to receive the medal and the ribbon. An elegant and beautiful lady, tall, plump and fair, accompanied her to the dais.

After the ceremony, the elegant lady, tall, plump, and fair, came to Vimla to express her feelings. 'My pride doubles when I escort someone from our region to receive such a high honour. I am the Secretary of Internal Security. I am from Rewari.'

'Our village is close to Rewari. In fact my husband was in KPS College for one year.'

'I did my graduation from there. Which year was he in KPS?'

'I have no idea of that. I only know that he fell in love with a girl there and was badly beaten up for the audacity. He offended the girl and could never come to terms with his guilt.'

An uncanny wave suddenly swept Gurmeet's mind.

'I knew a boy but his name had something to do with buffaloes I remember.'

'Actually our surname is *dasbhainsiya* but my husband found it very embarrassing and officially removed it from his name. We gujjars traditionally mend buffaloes.'

Gurmeet was shell-shocked for a moment. She pulled herself to come out of this bizarre feeling. Took out her visiting card and gave to Vimla.

'You must come to my house whenever you visit Rewari. I will be very happy.' She was abrupt. Something was swirling inside her. She begged for Vimla's leave.

She went straight to the bath room to wash up her face. Her eyes were welled up.

Whole night she tried to remember where she had kept that piece of paper. She was sure it was somewhere in her belongings. After so many years it was not possible to recall and she was not ready to give up.

Vimla visited Gurmeet's house one day; a big palatial *kothi*. She took Bheem along with her. Gurmeet was overjoyed to see Vimla and her son. She told her daughter to take Bheem to her room and show him how to play a computer game.

'Bheem is a very quiet boy.' Gurmeet was pensive.

'Like his father.' Vimla was prompt.

'Yes, like his father.' Vimla was amused to hear.

Gurmeet's daughter came running to complain, 'Mom, I don't want to play with Bheem. He is not playing at all. He's all the time staring at me. He's not a good boy.'

'Gurmeet flared up, suddenly.'

'No Meet, don't talk like this, he's a very nice boy. He's staring at you doesn't mean you can call him a bad boy. Go and be nice with him.'

'Don't be so angry madam, she doesn't mean anything, she is a pretty child.'

There was a pause before the two resumed their talk.

'What's your daughter's name, Meet?'

Her name is actually Manmeet Kaur. Meet is her nick name.

They were together the whole afternoon. Gurmeet wanted to know every small thing of Chiman's life. The thought Vimla could easily guess the truth of past was coming to her in flashes.

'Your husband loved poetry.' Gurmeet went in trance.

I still remember the last line of a poem he wrote, '*You will be there with me/There with me, you will be*'

She was suddenly aware. 'Let's have one more cup of tea.'

'No, tell me more about his time in college. He never told me about this poem.' Vimla was sincerely curious.

'Wish I knew more.' Gurmeet had moisture in her eyes.

Silence prevailed. It was broken when Meet came scurrying into the drawing room, Bheem chasing behind.

'Mom, can I give my computer game to Bheem, he now knows how to play with it.'

'You are such a nice girl.' Gurmeet kissed her gladly.

Bheem was standing at a distance.

'Come here my son!' Gurmeet desired to hug him.

Vimla was lost in her thoughts.

THANK YOU, RUK!

A good human being is one who unflinchingly believes in the stupidity called love. I am not I am sure. I doubt she is.

Not very affectionate but she is a responsible wife. May not be a dream husband still I am also not a difficult partner. We have heard others say, and that can't be without a reason, that we make a nice and happy couple. We do take care of each other. And the life is good, by and large. In spite of all the good part, for some reason or the other, we get into those silly husband-wife arguments often climaxing into a silence of conflict. It happens once in a while but does, without fail. All direct communication, barring the objectively essential, crashes down in a flicker.

The patch-up moment comes after a week or sometimes two, triggered by something very mundane. At the end, the 'canonical' viewpoint that kicked it off vanishes, exposing the stupidity that dragged it without a rationale. I believe she too thinks the same once it gets over. Earlier, at every reconciliation, I would think a day will come this inanity will taper out. And we will be a perfect couple. But no, it seems preordained. Looks it will continue until one of us is not there to take part in this wordless clash. And there is a probability that the moment of final departure comes right in the middle of one such silent war. That, if happens, will really cause an insufferable pain to the one who stays back to live. The thought makes me shudder.

If it is I who opts every time to go into the shell first then she can't escape the responsibility of pushing the button. Losing temper is not the issue. I am no saint. Anger is one thing and that venomous look is altogether different. I am talking about that stare of few seconds that instantly shatters the relationship of twenty years into innumerable pieces of unbearable moments. That look and only that murderous look is what turns the usual bickering into a war of no words. That is where the life comes to a screeching halt. This emotionless cold stare throws me far back into time, straight into the mesmeric hug of my aunt. Her name was Rukmini.

She was my aunt, not real still close. Today I would like to call her Ruk, just Ruk! This is for a mix of reasons I have harboured in my mind. The obvious one is that when I saw her last she was a few years younger than I am today. But there is one more reason, predominant and pivotal. And I am quite sure that this one undoubtedly allows me to call her Ruk.

I was raw, just a kid of five; too young to know what really all that was. Time has gone but that experience has stayed with me and is still fresh in my mind. Ruk had her reason—a very strong reason to see me die. I would know it much later. At that tender age I overwhelmingly loved to be into that magic wrap. My death was the only way for her to win over her most despicable rival in life. My mother. She hated my mother from the bottom of her heart. The reason was me. My mother had a big plus in me against the stigma of infertility Ruk was living with. There was perhaps no other way for poor Ruk to resurrect herself.

The moment she saw me she would leap upon me like a desperate lover. She did it loudly, if my mother was around. She would clasp my head between her two silky palms and shower me with heaps of blessings. Her next immediate move would be to look into my eyes. And this was the look I was talking—a look that always overstayed for few seconds before turning into a lethal stare. I find it blank as death when I recall it now. To my innocent mind, it was a dose of love.

Ruk won't stop here. I would wait for her next move with a bated breath, my gaze fixed at my destination— the deep gorge in between her two fabulous breasts. She knew my mind, I guess. She would fondle my head to make me ready for the deep dive, still staring into my eyes. As she would shove my head into her gorgeous valley, my small hands clamped to her plump waist. It still seems so blissful. I always craved to feel that warmth for longer. But that was not allowed. My mother always created a reason to snatch me away from her. At times she would be ready to take me away before Ruk even made her attempt. Decades have passed but that feeling of ecstasy is still alive in me.

From my mother's murmur I would imagine that Ruk was up to something terrible, something very upsetting. I never believed but. I found my mother's anger unfounded until I knew the truth. That was much later. At this point in time I was just in love with Ruk. So much that I would come running to be in her arms the moment I heard her voice.

Ruk had nothing against me except that I was a male child born out of the womb of a sworn rival of hers. She agonizingly yearned to see my mother howling on the dead body of her only son. She wished to see my mother more unfortunate and wretched than a woman who could never be a mother. My death was the only way.

Ruk would be in tears sometimes while playing this deadly game of love with me. My heart would go out for her.

I don't think if at any time she made any attempt to kill me. No, I doubt Ruk could ever do something like that. To me, never.

Her wish remained unfulfilled and I grew up to understand her hidden desire. The dead blank look behind her glowing cheeks, whenever I recalled, came as a testimony of her intent to see me dead. Still I could never hate her. I rather empathized with her. Ruk had a reason, a very strong reason after all.

But this woman is my wife. I am everything to her. How can she give me the same stare of death?

A silly squabble and I face the same bloody stare. It has happened once again. I have not spoken a word to her since then. I can't. It just makes me withdraw from the piece of happy life I do otherwise comfortably share with her. She too won't blink.

It's past midnight. She is sleeping or may be just lying with her face to the wall. I am not sure.

'You are dead, Ruk. My mother too passed away long ago. I believe this woman loves me. She had problems with my mother. But that was nothing more than usual feminine envy. She would never wish me death, I know, though that look in her eyes is unquestionably the same. It seems that you have only given it to her. She has the right to be angry with me. Every wife has. But how can she wish me dead, Ruk?'

So engrossed I was that I unmindfully soliloquised my thoughts in a low tone.

'I have thought of it a lot. I want an answer from you, Ruk.' I whispered. My heart only heard.

'When it comes to woman, you are still a kid of five, my love. You won't ever understand a woman. She is not just what I was to you; she doesn't wish death to you. You don't have an idea how ferociously she wants to protect you. It is her dilemma; she wants a complete possession of your life, including your death. Understand her pain.' I heard a voice that came from the loneliness of the dark night. It was muffled but I could clearly make out after decades of I heard it last. It was Ruk's.

I looked around. The shadow of palm tree danced on the wall. Moon had travelled a long stretch of the empty sky and looked tired.

I looked at my wife. She was still sleeping in the same position on a mattress spread on the floor just beside the bed. She always sleeps like this when angry. She has unknowingly picked up a few of my mother's habits but only after my mother passed away.

It reminds me my mother. She too slept on a mattress mostly with her face to the wall, particularly when she had to show her annoyance.

'I am not sure whether she is sleeping or is just lying with her eyes closed, Ruk.' I believed Ruk was still there somewhere in that darkness.

'She will not come to me as I know she has indefatigable patience, Ruk! Or in these matters women don't need what men call patience. They are just like that. I will only have to break this silence, I know.'

'I think I should go and sleep next to her as I did when my mother was angry with me. I don't know how she will react.'

She might pretend to be in sleep for some time. I am feeling like putting my hand over her soft and plump waist. I really don't know. She might throw my hand away and scold, 'Go and sleep in your bed, I am not well.'

My mother often did so.

'She may not make any movement for some time to see my fingers pleadingly moving from one part to another of her body. She turns then perhaps. I would like to believe. She

might hold my head into her hands, look into my face for a few seconds, and shove me in between her two gorgeous breasts, without speaking a word. Like you always did to me after your words of blessings were over. I will clamp her waist tightly in response. Words will join tomorrow when the day begins.'

'Now it is dark, Ruk!'

Moonlight is filtering through the window making a patch of light on the wall and the shadow of palm tree is still dancing in that spotlight.

'In this darkness I don't know you are still around or gone. In this darkness I will not be able to see if she will have your stare in her eyes or not.'

'I am dying to take a deep plunge in that 'valley of death'. I will not be able to see its overwhelming profundity, the way I saw yours without batting my eyelids. But I will more intensively feel its tranquillity and warmth. Let death be there waiting for me.'

'You are gone it seems, Ruk.'

But I must say—*'no matter you wished me death; you also taught me love. Thank you, Ruk!'*

A FOOL'S PROMISE

I will be late, very soon. I am 77. There is no reason for me to pose smart now.

It all began when I was 17. She was a year or two younger to me. I was in search of love. It sometimes doesn't beget so easily; one has to really work hard to make it happen. People tend to construct a fanciful lie around it, once the pathetic phase is over. The strong intoxication of love cuts the bad piece of memory out. And here too, harsher the drink higher is the kick, like in alcohol.

Urgency and hopelessness made me close in on her. Convenience did me in. She was a neighbour. Love not conveyed is love not invited. I must admit that like most of the mortals, I too was looking for someone to love me. Falling in love is not a primary instinct, it's a condition precedent, one must fulfil. Making an advance was imperative on my part. So I did.

The time of dusk and the lonely corner of the veranda came in tandem to lift up my spirits. I tried to hug her. My fear made it look like a clumsy attempt of molestation. She was frightened. Her frightened look frightened me, and the result was, I stopped half way. She gave me a smile before scurrying away.

I read that smile on her face or misread it I am not sure till date. To me, it spelt l . . . o . . . v . . . e; something happened and I promised to myself—'I love her.'

I saw the elaboration of that smile when she turned to look back. There was no doubt. Holding that feeling tightly I escaped to the outskirts of the town. I needed to be away from everything else. I was in love. It took me a while to soak it up.

I came home late that evening. How would I know that my long absence was going to be a piece of clinching evidence against me?

I found something eerie in the air as I entered our lane. Untowardness had left its footprints in the air. The looks that came from doors and windows were setting a prelude for the tongues to find suitable tones and words. My mind had sensed the trouble and it went into the shell. Heart was left alone to beat the retreat.

I could hear the sound of my footsteps and my heart beats as I entered our door. Suddenly there was a din behind me. Selected voices were taking lead, I heard.

My mother suddenly covered me as if there was going to be an attack on me. She pulled me into the kitchen and closed the door.

Something awful was happening here, I realized, when I was on with the wings I got a few hours back. My mind came back, and I tried to summarize the utterances, I just heard.

Her parents came to our door and abused my parents. She had hidden herself in some corner after complaining that I tried to do something outrageous to her. My parents ferociously defended me but the audacious stand did nothing but heightened the row. My father and her father got physical. Her father gave a tight slap to my father. My father picked up a rod and hit that on her father's head. People separated the two but the damage was done. Her father's head was bleeding profusely. It was going to be a police case had my mother not gone and pleaded for their mercy. My father allowed her to do her best to save the residual honour.

After a short lull, another round of abuses came, this time aimed at me than my parents. The adjectives used were—Characterless . . . ! Rascal . . . ! A blot on the family . . . etc, to single me out and not like Bastard! Ill-bred . . . ! That was perhaps to exonerate my parentage. There was not a whisper from our side in return. For some reason my father spared me. It was surprising.

Thanks to some worldly wise neighbours, the matter was settled with a decision—'It wouldn't be forgiven if happens again.' The wise intervention somehow bailed us out but failed to save the ties between two decent neighbours.

Actually nothing had happened between me and her. And if prodded she would have clarified, I believed. I just made an advance, and that went awry.

It was actually I who should have felt betrayed. The smile, I am still sure, was not fallacious.

That apart, what about the promise I made to myself in those two hours. You can't break a promise you make to yourself. I reiterated to myself—'Come what may, I love her.'

I was suddenly a curious character in the neighbourhood. This incident thereafter became an essential part of my introduction, in any conversation I figured. If some girls behaved as if cold shouldering me was a proof of their immaculate character there were others who looked at me like wanted to say, 'Don't take it to your heart, that flat-nosed witch hardly deserves a boy like you.' Then there were women who never failed to show the expression of amazement—'I can't believe this' every time they saw me passing by. By feigning ignorance to what was happening around me I unwittingly enhanced their fun. Men gave me the peculiar look of consolation—'No big deal, it happens. It happens with every one, just be careful in future.' Loafers of the neighbourhood now gave me a nod of recognition. Ready to take all this in my stride, I just wanted to see her reaction after this episode, to know the fate of that smile.

She managed timing of her ins and outs in a way that I couldn't see her for months. As the matter cooled off I saw her a few times with her friends. It was difficult to say whether she saw me or not.

Then came a day we faced each other in a long shot—a long empty lane between us. Not to embarrass her I kept my gaze down till she came quite close. I looked up only once to see if she was looking at me or not.

She was. She had the extension of the same fucking smile on her face. I looked at her with dispassion to convey—'I don't care for you and your smile, because I am sure that I love you. And that's it.'

I didn't know what she took it as. There was no question of either of us going beyond exchanging those inexplicable looks for the next three years. In view of the background, a slight move on either side was enough to set the street ablaze.

Three years went like that.

I was twenty and a graduate. I was set to leave the town for two years to do my post-graduation. Only one thing was sure that she would be married off on one of those seven hundred odd days of the two years. A couple of weeks were left to my departure and I was whiling away with my college friends with that edginess in mind—'Hey guys, we don't know when we will meet again.' Life was to play a game of 'go away till you meet again' it seemed. So the time was to remain together as much as you can.

I returned home late. As I was about to enter, her parents came out of my house. We had not spoken to any one from their family after the weird incident. They ignored me as if it had nothing to do with me. My mother gave me a smile, a teaser to guess the answer of the very simple puzzle just put to me. I was blank.

She asked me to come to the kitchen.

'What you think we don't have any clue? You have been trying to make a fool of us but we are your parents, my dear. We had inkling and now they have confirmed that you like her and she also likes you.'

I couldn't believe my ears. I didn't know where it all came from. But whatever was said on my behalf was true. I loved her. I was really a fool, I reminded myself.

We got engaged after a few months. We got married after two years.

We lived together for 55 years, really a long time.

Whenever I told her that I tried to hug you because I loved you. Her reply came with the same smile.

'I don't believe so. Had I let you have your way, perhaps it would have gotten over that day itself. Girls don't fall in love. They are not fools like boys are.'

I think she was right. A girl never makes a promise to herself. She simply loves.

She passed away last year. I am keeping my fool's promise. No regrets.

PREMONITION

She balked at his witticism and he endured her attitude. Before they could sort out, aversion had tripped into infatuation. A month after their first face-off in a conference at The Taj they were in bed at Sonia's house. Rajiv was Sonia's boss.

Sexually enterprising Sonia is no more. She is more in Rajiv's mind now.

Sonia bewitched Rajiv. He pampered her waywardness. It was an exciting ride till Medha instinctively discovered this muse in his life. Sonia cuckolded her hubby. The affair was rapturous still not worth risking conjugal rewards, both knew; Rajiv more.

Rajiv sought to steer clear of the mess while Sonia wished to sail with the winds.

'We need to end it, Sonia. Medha has come to know', Rajiv imploringly spoke to her on the phone.

Sonia rolled with laughter. 'Not we Rajiv, you have to end it.'

'How about ending at where we began, the Taj', she rejoined.

They came back to The Taj for an elegant split. She was jovial as ever. For Rajiv, the party was over.

Rajiv was looking sideways for the words while Sonia amusingly watched his embarrassment.

Staccato . . . It was a sound of gunshots.

Sonia sprang up to cover Rajiv and suddenly collapsed over Rajiv's right arm. A bullet had hit her head; a blob of blood dropped on his left wrist. Rajiv was frozen.

Wantonly spraying bullets, a baby-faced monster dashed upstairs.

Commotion brought Rajiv to his feet. Wiping blood off his wrist, Rajiv gaped at her calm face. Within a minute he was out with the throng. The enormity left him blank.

'I am driving home . . . Yes, there is tension . . . Yes, it looks like terrorist attack . . .' Medha was on the line.

It was 26/11/2008.

For the next two days people were glued to their TV sets.

'That bitch is also Hussain, right?' Medha was watching news.

'It's Sonia only', he murmured.

'Thank God, I reined you in time; sheer premonition.' she slumped in the sofa.

SALVATION

She appeared all of a sudden. 'How are you doing, my son?'

In the mess I was, it was embarrassing to face her.

'How come you are here, Ma? This is not the place you should be meeting me, and that too after such a long time', hesitatingly I asked.

'I know you are having a bad dream and I have barged in from nowhere. It has been really long, my son, you had me in your dream, though I am glad you still think of me quite often.' She looked tired yet calm.

Her words evoked guilt in me but the realization it was happening in a dream was relieving.

'Where were you all these days?' I expressed my concern.

She smiled. 'Oh! You are not able to comprehend, my poor child. No real space for me, I have just two places to live in—thoughts and dreams. I died a few years ago, son! You are having a dream. You are unable to grasp the reality at this moment.'

Piercing through my perplexity, she continued, 'It's going to be less and less, far and far. It might take some decades before I am completely forgotten. No thoughts for me; no dreams for me. They will be your abode then.'

'And then?' I was petrified.

'Then it's salvation! My son, salvation! Don't be so scared, it comes after long years', she said with a pale smile before disappearing.

I was suddenly awake. Wide awake.